HER NAME IS GRACE

Her Name Is Grace

by

HOWARD E. CROUCH

Published by
The Damien-Dutton Society for Leprosy Aid, Inc.
616 Bedford Avenue, Bellmore, New York 11710
U.S.A.
www.damienleprosysociety.org

International Standard Book Number: 0–9606330–7–3
Library of Congress Number: 2003106031
Published by the Damien-Dutton Society for Leprosy Aid, Inc.
616 Bedford Avenue, Bellmore, New York 11710
Printed in the United States of America

DEDICATION

This book is dedicated to the two Betty's,
Betty Campbell and Betty Lanigan.
Like many of my previous books,
the two Betty's are responsible for much of the research,
transposing from my garbled tapes to the written page,
and the final manuscript.
This book in particular was the most difficult.
With the loss of most of my eyesight
everything had to be read to me.
They spent hours typing, retyping and retyping again.
Only their many years of dedication
to the cause of the Damien-Dutton Society
kept them from throwing the entire project
into the wastebasket.
Their patience, their understanding,
and especially their encouragement
are responsible for the publication of this book.
I am eternally grateful for their support.

Books by Howard E. Crouch

Her Name Is Grace
Brother Dutton of Molokai
Damien and Dutton, Two Josephs on Molokai
This One Is For Gussie

Books by co-authors
Howard E. Crouch and Sister Mary Augustine, smsm

After Damien: Dutton
Two Hearts, One Fire
Once Over and Lightly

ACKNOWLEDGEMENTS

It is always a difficult task to list those whom you wish to acknowledge as being helpful in the preparation of the manuscript. You are bound to leave someone out, and if I have, I apologize.

In addition to the two Betty's to whom this book is dedicated, I am grateful to Terry Baldassi and Carol Tufano for the many hours they spent in reading each word back to me, correcting and rearranging words to make the text meaningful.

To Juliette Hanks and Esther Meyers for their expertise in proofreading and their helpful suggestions to bring cohesion to the story.

I thank the remainder of my dedicated staff at Damien-Dutton, Terry Donnelly, Rose Rampanelli and Ellen Russo for their patience and understanding in bringing this book to fruition.

All profits from the sale of this book will be given to the Damien-Dutton Society for Leprosy Aid, Inc.

PROLOGUE

THE EVENTS IN THIS STORY took place more than 60 years ago. In some cases I have used fictitious names to protect the privacy of those involved. During the time when these events took place the word leper was still widely used. It is an odious word, stigmatizing the victim of this ancient and dread disease. Leprosy is a viable medical term, since it describes the disease and not a person. There are some who prefer to use the term Hansen's disease, named after a Norwegian scientist by the name of Doctor Gerhard Hansen, who discovered the causative agent of leprosy, commonly named the *mycobacterium leprae.* I believe by using the term Hansen's disease, it indicates that Dr. Hansen had leprosy which he never did have. I apologize to those victims of this disease for using the odious term.

For the reader who knows little about leprosy, it is one of the earliest diseases known to mankind and often in the Bible there are many references to leprosy and its victims. There have been some dramatic changes in recent years particularly after the discovery of the sulfones in the 1940's. Up until that time the only known treatment was chaulmoogra oil, obtained from the nut of a tree that grew in India but it was ineffective in the majority of cases. The early sulfones had some modicum of success but not all victims responded until the recent use of several drugs known as multiple drug therapy. This has been effective in arresting the disease if the patient is treated in its early stages. It cannot correct the deformities and the loss of parts of the body that have occurred. Many people, including well-known scientists and health organization workers declare that leprosy is cured. I am in the minority but I prefer the word arrested. The word cured to me denotes that the disease will never return. Yet, it has re-occurred in some cases where the multiple drug therapy was very successful. Today, there are over 800,000 new cases reported each year and the incidence of children has more than doubled. Leprosy has been found in almost every country of the world including the United States.

There are still many unanswered questions and one of the tragic results of announcing that leprosy will soon be eradicated is the significant drop in funds for the care of the more than 15 million people still suffering from leprosy. The figures vary, as it is difficult to diagnose and report each individual case and standards for reporting are not uniform. Another result of the premature news is that there are fewer and fewer workers to assist in caring for the present victims who have leprosy and fewer dedicated researchers, not only have leprosy hospitals closed but research labs as well. Those still engaged in the efforts to conquer leprosy are handicapped by lack of funds to continue the search for a vaccine, which is the ultimate answer to the conquest of leprosy. If a vaccine is found that will prevent the disease it will eventually eradicate it and we can say in all honesty that leprosy has been cured. That is the goal of the Damien-Dutton Society for Leprosy Aid as long as there are concerned people willing to make personal sacrifices to finish the task.

CHAPTER ONE

IT WAS A SUNDAY IN AUGUST OF 1941 that the *SS Siboney* slipped through the narrow passageway into the wide harbor of Kingston, Jamaica, British West Indies. The sun was shining brightly as we stood at the rail and watched the sprawling city come into view, nestled on a strip of land at the base of a range of mountains. We had spent five days sailing from New York aboard this former luxury liner, now converted into a troop ship. There were more than 200 GI's on board. We were not told until the night before our docking, what our destination was to be. We were not at war but the Atlantic and the Caribbean were filled with U-Boats seeking to destroy any vessel carrying cargo or supplies for the Allies. We were to occupy an Army Base as a result of an agreement known as the Lend-Lease Act. President Franklin Roosevelt and Winston Churchill arranged it in return for us supplying England with ships and war material. The Act aroused the anger of Germany and its Allies.

Just a few months before my arrival, I had been drafted into the Army and shipped to Camp Lee, Virginia. I was to complete a 13–week basic training course as an Army Medic. Several weeks before the course was to be completed, I was called out of ranks and told to prepare my duffel bag and was shipped back to Fort Dix which was just 30 miles from my home in New Brunswick, New Jersey. Overjoyed, I thought I would be located close to my home, but I never got to see my parents, for the day after I arrived at Fort Dix, I was shipped out aboard the *Siboney.* I only had time for a call home. I was a replacement for a regular Army Medic who had broken his leg just prior to sailing.

As we moored at the docks we could see the streets of downtown Kingston, crowded with buildings, many of them no more than shacks. In the main business district there was one large, wide paved street with buildings made of cement and wood, not higher than two stories, with corrugated iron or tin roofs. The city had known devastation from fires and hurricanes over the course of its existence. Beyond the main part of the city were the suburbs where there were more modest bungalow homes surrounded by gardens. Further from the city were the slums, consisting of small shacks, some with tin roofs and others covered by palm fronds where the poor were crowded together. In stark contrast, the Blue Mountains were covered with lush greens and dotted with substantial homes. It was nearly noon and the sun was at its zenith. Despite the heat there was a cool breeze blowing in from the Caribbean. We were ordered to line up in formation on the open decks to greet the Governor General and other dignitaries who boarded the ship. We were the first contingent of American troops to land in Jamaica. The British, Canadian and Australian troops had already arrived. Jamaica was chosen for its strategic position to guard the Panama Canal. The canal was the focal point for a pack of U-Boats awaiting the arrival of freighters as they passed through carrying war goods.

It was all strange and exotic to me for I had never left the States. We prepared to disembark. First the Army jeeps, trucks, ambulances and other vehicles followed by the troops. We boarded the trucks and jeeps forming a convoy headed out of town. As we passed through the main street I noticed there were very few cars. The principal means of transportation seemed to be the trolleys whose tracks ran down the middle of the road. The various shops fascinated me. Some were modern with colonnades and roofing covering the sidewalk so that one would be walking in the shade. Some shops featured goods from England, such as china, leather goods and silverware. While others from the mid-east and the Orient carried fine silks, ivory and other exotic merchandise. What caught my eye was a pharmacy with an ice cream parlor attached which had a long counter with tables and chairs just like back home. Then there was a Post Office and several banks and a theatre advertising a coming pantomime. Most of the pedestrians going in and out of the shops and strolling along the street were well dressed. Men in white linen suits and women fashionably dressed with all shapes, sizes and colors of hats. It was evident that the poor could not afford this neighborhood. I was wondering when I would have the chance to spend some time here.

Soon we were on the outskirts of the city and the contrast was stark. There were large plots of land covered with huts of every size and description. Only the main road was paved. The side streets were dusty. There were a few small shops selling a variety of merchandise and bearing Chinese names. One amused me as it had a sign hanging from the roof, which said, hardware, utensils, dry goods and etc. Standing outside of the shop were several wooden coffins for sale. From birth to death, all under one roof, I thought.

We were now on the open road. Here the foliage thickened with numerous trees lining the road. I could see in the far distance a range of high mountains. With the thick foliage it seemed as if there was little habitation until you passed by an opening in the trees and could see beyond little cottages and huts. The road was crowded with vehicles of every kind, most of them carts drawn either by oxen, mules or donkeys. On our side of the road most of them were empty as they had already delivered their produce for markets in Kingston and were returning to their farms and plantations. On the other side there were carts headed towards Kingston piled high with bananas, sugar cane, vegetables, fruits and merchandise of every description. Following along were many women, their heads piled with more products. They all looked tall and straight. No bent backs as they carried the load on their head. In some carts were men with whips, cracking them over the heads of the oxen, who seemed to pay little attention until the whip reached their flesh. I cringed at what seemed to me to be cruelty but I soon learned that the poor people of Jamaica took all of their frustration out on their poor animals. Here and there one could see a stray goat and even the dogs looked emaciated and cowering.

We were now in the Parish of St. Catherine. Jamaica was divided up into Parishes. Most of them were named after Saints, which was strange since there were few Catholics in Jamaica. As we traveled along the Spanish Town road heading northward we came to a small wooden bridge spanning the Rio Cobre, one of the most beautiful rivers I have ever seen. It was a fast moving river, shallow along its banks and deeper near its center. Fed by mountain streams it twisted and curved as it made its way to the sea. In the middle of the river the water moved rapidly. Larger rocks were scattered along its bed and the water splashed against the rocks cascading into miniature waterfalls. At its shallow banks it was so clear that one could see its white sandy bottom. The colors varied as if from an artist's palette. Depending on the depth of the sunlight, it ranged from emerald green along the banks to azure blue, turquoise and dark green where there were shadows from the overhanging trees. Lining both banks were acacia trees, royal poinciana, mahogany and coconut palms and at intervals large cottonwood trees forming an overhead arch. In between grew colorful and flowering bushes, vines and honeysuckle and beds of wild violets. The air was cool, moist and scented with the smell of fresh lemons from the lemon grass that grew in profusion. I watched groups of small children, all naked, ranging in colors from pale white to ebony black. They were splashing and whooping with glee. The road was hot and dusty and I longed to remove my sweaty Army uniform to jump in and join in the fun.

As if the head of the convoy read our minds, trucks, jeeps and lorries pulled off and parked on the side of the road. We were told that we would have an hour. So we scrambled out. To the right was a road leading to Spanish Town. We were anxious to stretch our legs. It was a ten-minute walk to the town for those who wished to visit it briefly. I wanted to see everything and I took off. Soon I entered the town, which was once the capitol of Jamaica when the Spaniards had conquered the island. There were many shops and we all headed to the soda fountain where there was cold coke and ice cream. Tall buildings which once housed the government, the legislature, the governor's residence, the cathedral, and the courthouse made up the square. In the middle was a small park with beautiful trees and a fountain but the streets were almost empty. It seemed like the town was deserted. I went to a shop selling souvenirs and books and picked up a volume on the history of Jamaica. I wanted to know as much of my new home as would be possible. It was hot and we trudged back to the trucks yearning for a dip but we had no time and we boarded again. Natives had gathered around the convoy and I struck up a conversation with one of the men who spoke clear English. I guessed he was some official. He told us that the town would always be open to us whenever we could leave our Base. I pointed to the road on the other side leading back into a large group of trees.

I asked him, "What was beyond that road?"

And he said, "You don't want to go there, son. That road leads to the leper colony."

Ye gods, I thought, lepers' - that was one disease that I had not anticipated encountering. Fevers, yes, but not leprosy. I did not know it then that I would often travel that road and spend many hours at the Leprosarium.

The driver of my truck was a tall muscular young man in his middle 30's wearing the uniform of the Army Corps of Engineers. He introduced himself as Roy. I asked him where his home was and he said, "Texas." He had been working on the Base for the last six months and I was glad to have someone who would give me some information. We passed many huge banana plantations. He told me that the banana trees grew to be 10 to 12 feet tall. The trunk was very soft and was about a foot in diameter and could easily be cut with the swipe of a machete. At the top the fruit began to grow in large bunches, the bananas facing upward, and as they matured the weight would bend the tree. It was one of Jamaica's most abundant exports to England. On the other side of the road were huge sugar plantations and the canes were swaying gracefully in the wind. Men and women were hacking away and cutting down the stalks, carrying them to carts, where mules waited patiently until the carts were filled. They would then be taken to the sugar mills, some to be used to make raw sugar, others to make rum, both of which were another product that the island exported. It was backbreaking work and most of the workers were gleaming with sweat.

I asked Roy whether the workers were paid well and he said, "No, it is almost like slave labor. They work for a few pence."

He said that when the Corps of Engineers arrived to survey the land that was to become the Army Base and an Air Field for both Navy reconnaissance planes and bombers, the area was filled with wild brush. The soil was sandy and the area lay in the gully, thus it was named Sandy Gully. To the north we could see more clearly the mountains but they were not like the Blue Mountains of Kingston. They seemed to be white and he explained most of it was limestone. The mountains were ringed with many precipices and they were so tall that we could not even see the top, which was covered in clouds.

He said, "It is called Mount Diablo, the devil's mountain, because of its hairpin turns and accidents were frequent on the mountain roads."

One could see many waterfalls. Roy explained that the mountains of Jamaica made it different from the other islands of the Caribbean. Not only did they add beauty but also they were the source of abundant water, especially during the rainy season, which lasted several months. They formed many rivers and streams throughout the island, which helped in the vegetation and the growing of crops. It also afforded sites of beauty, luring tourists from around the world. Luxury hotels with sandy beaches were scattered along the coastline.

"Many of them were empty," Roy said, "because the royalty and wealthy of Europe were restricted from traveling to the island and many cruise ships were converted into troop ships."

The tourists were a major source of income for the Jamaicans who served as housemaids, waiters and yard boys for the resorts.

He said, "When the Corps of Engineers first came to survey the land and to begin to clear it for the building of the Base, word spread like wildfire through the island, stating that they would be hiring many workers to build the Base." He blew the horn to scatter the goats on the road.

He turned to me and said, "It created a lot of tension with the government because we were paying as much as three and four times what Jamaican labor was making."

They gathered up their tools and headed for the Gully seeking employment, leaving businesses, hotels and homes without the much needed yard boys, cooks and maids. Few were skilled, so many were turned away and eventually the government made an agreement with American officials to lower the pay so that there would be little competition between the Jamaican government and the Americans. The Corps of Army Engineers brought their families. They were a rough and ready group and the upper class Englishmen avoided them. They were not invited into the social strata of the island.

CHAPTER TWO

NOW WE COULD SEE THE beginning of the Base. A tall chain link fence surrounded on top with sharp barbed wire lined the road. Beyond the barbed wire was a sprawling expanse of barrack like buildings. They stood on cement blocks, which Roy told me was to prevent flooding during the rainy season, which inundated the gully. It also kept the crawling insects from entering the barracks. Some buildings were about 20 feet in length, others longer. All had steps leading up to the entrance to the barracks. Others had shaded walks between them. We were nearing the gate of the Fort, which I now knew was called Fort Simonds. The streets inside were filled with jeeps, trucks, cranes, bulldozers, plows and vehicles of every sort and hundreds of Jamaicans busy hammering away on ladders. A railroad siding was built from the one track that passed through parts of the countryside. The main track led into Kingston with several spurs into the various plantations by which freight trains would carry bags of sugar and other produce to the ports of Kingston. The boxcars, Roy told me, were a means of transportation for workers from the various towns and villages near the Base. Others came by bicycle, on foot, or riding mules or donkeys. On the right hand side of the road opposite the Base, beyond large trees, could be seen a sprawling shantytown, similar to the ones we saw as we left the capitol of Kingston. Beyond that I could see a flowing river. Roy explained to me that it was called the Milk River. It was fed by mountain streams and flowed southward to the sea. While we were waiting at the gate, I spied a little girl, hunched over a straw basket of fruit, on the side of the road leading to the shantytown. She was dressed in clean but shabby clothes with a red bandana on her head. Her face was beautiful, her expression sad. I wondered who she was. Little did I know then that she would play an important role in my life in Jamaica.

Finally, we entered the gates to the Base. There were MP soldiers manning the guardhouse who checked all of the credentials. Roy told me that they had arrived earlier by plane along with members of the command staff to take over the duties of guarding the Base from the local constabulary, which had been hired by the United States Government. As we passed through I was impressed by many of the small barracks with grassy lawns in front and flowerbeds and a covered porch running alongside. There were children playing in the yards. Roy told me that many of the Army Engineers had brought their wives and families with them. These barracks were provided as living quarters and were composed of two bedrooms, bath, a large living room, a kitchen and a den, amply furnished and stocked with linens. All this would be turned over to the officers of the Base Command once the Engineers had left. Roy had asked me what unit I was with and I told him the Medical Corps.

He said, "You will be housed temporarily in the small barracks to serve as a hospital until the engineers leave when you will take over the large Base hospital composed of several buildings and fully equipped as an operating unit."

The trucks pulled into a circular drive in front of the Command Headquarters. A tall flagpole at the entrance to the headquarters building was flying the Stars and Stripes. This land now belonged to the United States. We left our trucks and jeeps and lined up in formation to be greeted by the Commanding Officer of the Base, Colonel Ewing and his staff. Using a microphone he welcomed us to Fort Simonds. A thin man in a white suit, with a white starched collar attached to a black vest, was introduced as Father Philip Kiely of the Jesuit Order who was pastor of the Catholic Chapel in May Pen. He would serve as our temporary Base Chaplain until our regular chaplain would arrive. This was a man who was to change my life forever. After that, the commanding officer of each of the various contingents called out our names. We shouldered our duffle bags and followed them to our quarters. Our commander was Captain Holland, M.D. and his assistant, a Lieutenant. Rosenberg, M.D. We walked to what was to become our temporary hospital, which was only a few hundred yards from the Command Headquarters. It consisted of three small buildings connected with an open walkway between them and beyond the third was a cement-block building which, we found out, was our bathroom and showers. First of the three buildings was the offices of the medical staff, a clinic and a supply room. Connecting that was the hospital, which consisted of 15 beds. Next to that was the headquarters of the Medical Corps, composed of 16 GI's. I was placed in charge of the hospital because of my medical background and R.N. degree.

The patients' building was more like an Infirmary than a hospital. Anyone needing advanced medical care would be sent to the engineer's main hospital. We were shown to our bunks, each covered with a canopy of mosquito netting for insects were everywhere. We were each given a footlocker to store our personal belongings. Captain Holland and Lieutenant. Rosenberg greeted each of us personally and provided us with a cold bottle of Red Stripe beer, which everyone gulped thirstily. He then told us to wash up in the bathhouse and to line up in front where we would then be marched to the Mess Hall. We were all famished and it did not take long for us to wash up, line up and march to the Mess Hall. It reminded us very quickly that we were still in the Army. In the large common Mess Hall, there were sections set aside for the Army Engineers and their families, another for the officers and the rest of the hall for the enlisted men. Each had their own line to the steam tables. We each took a tray as we passed along the counter behind which stood servers in white uniforms. There was no choice, you took what you got and our plates were loaded with rice, vegetables, lamb stew, a heap of mashed potatoes, a plate of green salad, a piece of pie and your choice of beverage. It was not the Waldorf but the meal was tasty and very few plates had any food left. After the meal we lined up again and marched back to our barracks.

The sun had set but it was still light enough to see clearly. Captain Holland addressed us. He informed us that the evening would be free of duties and we would be confined to the hospital area. Taps would be at nine p.m. and all lights would be extinguished. He warned us that if we decided to go to the bathhouse we should check carefully in the corners of the cement floor for scorpions. The Captain passed around a bottle in which several scorpions were preserved in alcohol. The sting was at the tail and it contained poison that could kill or the pain would be so severe that you would wish that you were dead. Scorpions, we were told, hide in dark damp spaces. In the morning, we should check our boots for they find refuge in the damp toe of the boot. I shivered.

"Ye gods," I said again. "First lepers, now scorpions. What the hell did I get into!"

Captain Holland reminded us that reveille would be at six a.m. It did not take long for any of us to undress and crawl under the mosquito netting. Soon we heard the clear notes of taps followed by darkness as the lights were extinguished. The buzz of mosquitoes and insects trying hard to penetrate the netting to feed on our blood kept us awake. There were many different night sounds that I could not identify but within moments, my eyes closed and I was gone. I awoke several times during the night to hear snores throughout the barracks. Moonlight was filtering through the windows. I wanted to go to the bathroom but nothing would take me from beneath that netting to possibly step on a scorpion, so I waited until the morning. Oh, for a chamber pot! The night had cooled down as breezes came down from the mountain and a blanket was appreciated. Who would ever think of having a blanket in the tropics as Jamaica was blessed with comfortable weather for most of the year.

CHAPTER THREE

AS THE FIRST LIGHTS OF DAWN crept through the barracks windows, I could hear the creak of the freight train as it came into the siding and the sound of hundreds of voices, speaking in a tongue that I could not quite distinguish. The smell of burnt firewood wafted across the road from shantytown. It must be the natives preparing their breakfast, I thought.

Then came a large bang as the First Sergeant opened the door, switched on the lights and with a loud gruff voice, yelled, "Out of bed, out of bed. Up and at 'em."

I had not heard the bugler. We had twenty minutes to wash, shave, brush our teeth and be dressed to stand outside in formation. After roll call, we were told to break up and canvas the grounds to pick up any litter. I thought I was relieved of those duties after basic training but no, this became our daily routine. Then followed thirty minutes of calisthenics. The morning was cool so that was no problem. Then we marched to the Mess Hall. We had our choice of hot oatmeal or cold cereals, a dish of cut fresh fruit, bananas, oranges, pineapples, melons, and then came scrambled eggs, bacon, sausage, potatoes, toast and coffee. Most of the troops ate heartily for they faced a long hard day of labor. I was not used to such a big breakfast and ate sparingly but I soon learned that this was to keep you going for most of the rest of the day until the evening meal.

After breakfast we marched back to our barracks and assembled outside of Captain Holland's quarters. He told us what our mission was to be. This was a temporary hospital set-up and that we would be moving into the more sophisticated hospital now being occupied by the engineers. There would be a daily morning clinic for Army personnel with minor ailments, headache, diarrhea, sunburn, cuts, bruises and the like. Once every two weeks the entire Base command would line up to be inspected for any body lice or symptoms of venereal diseases. This was something new to me that I had seldom encountered in my hospital experience. Captain Holland told us that venereal diseases were rampant among the local people and even though we were forbidden to cross the road into shantytown there was always someone who would disobey the rules. If they were caught they were apprehended by the MP's and put in confinement. The disease had to be treated. In fact the first patient we had in our little infirmary, was a soldier with a virulent case of syphilis whom we had to keep in isolation and wear gowns and gloves when caring for him. Penicillin was not yet discovered so the major form of treatment was arsenic compound, which made the patient very ill. Five Corpsmen were assigned to me and we began to make up the beds in the hospital rooms, scrub the floors and walls and unpack equipment. One of the Corpsmen was a pharmacist, another a lab technician and a tough Irishman from Boston was a morgue technician. The others were aides, each with their own chores. During one of the breaks I studied the map of the Fort attached to one of the walls of the hospital room. I was surprised to see that there was a large swimming pool, an outdoor theatre for movies, another indoor theater for shows, an officer's club, a non-commissioned officer's club, a canteen and a post-exchange where you could purchase almost any article. There were toiletries, laundry and food. It was well stocked to supply the needs of the engineers' families.

CHAPTER FOUR

I LOCATED THE ENGINEERS' HOSPITAL, which would be our future home. It consisted of a cluster of eight long barracks connected with covered walks. One building was designated as the nurses' quarters. Civilian nurses from the local area who would leave once the engineers departed occupied it. When the Army nurses arrived they would be in that building. One building was designated as an operating room, scrub room, dental, pharmacy, laboratory, X-Ray and all of the other facilities of a well-equipped hospital. There were two buildings that contained patient beds. The sleeping quarters for the staff was in a separate building. There also was a building containing a large kitchen with a dining room for the staff and a preparation room for the patients' meals. I could not wait to move into this well laid out medical complex.

All day we could hear the cries of the hundreds of Jamaicans at the gate, begging for work and it reminded me of the deep Depression we in the States had just gone through. The days and weeks flew by and slowly the engineers departed. I was sorry to see Roy and his family go for I had spent many pleasant evenings with them and often I had been invited to supper.

By now I knew a great deal about the Jamaican people and their history. Finally, the Base had been completed. The last of the engineers had left and we moved into the new medical complex. Captain Holland notified me that I was promoted to the rank of Staff Sergeant. The officers now occupied the houses once occupied by the engineers and their families. A few lucky Jamaicans were hired to continue to take care of the grounds, to work in the laundry and the kitchens. Many of the officers kept on the housekeepers that the engineers had hired. Jamaican clerks and secretaries remained at their positions, freeing the Army from providing more personnel. In November, the first contingent of nurses arrived and much of my duty was lightened. There were six in all and they added a great deal to the ambiance of the Fort. They were not permitted to date or mingle with the enlisted men and there were many officers vying for their attention. Since I had my RN they treated me as an equal. The Chief Nurse had no objections when Captain Holland charged me with the supervision of the Operating Room.

CHAPTER FIVE

FATHER KIELY, WHO VISITED SEVERAL TIMES a week for Mass and on Sunday mornings, had become a good friend and we had long talks. One day he asked if I would like to accompany him to the Spanish Town Leprosarium, where he was scheduled to celebrate Mass. I fell silent and he looked at me with a slight grin.

"What's the matter, tough Sergeant?"

I blushed and stuttered, "Nothing, Father, nothing. Sure, I'll go."

"You can back out if you want to," he said.

That was a challenge that I could not resist. Absolutely not! "When do you want me to be ready?"

"I will pick you up at five o'clock next Saturday morning."

"I will have to get permission," I said.

"I will get it for you, don't worry."

He left with a twinkle in his eye. Sure enough he was there with his old Ford ready for me at five o'clock. I did not sleep well the night before, thinking that I would see people whose fingers would fall off and the germs permeating the air would infect me with leprosy. Despite these fears, I put on a brave front. The drive to Spanish Town at that time of the morning was easy as the roads were fairly empty. Most had brought their wares to the market on Friday night. We passed over the Rio Cobre, just as the sun was rising. Instead of turning left to Spanish Town, we turned right onto a long dusty road. The road was shaded with high trees and on one side we could see the sparkling waters of the river. Soon we came to the tall red brick wall that surrounded the Compound. My pulse rate increased. The moment of truth was at hand. How would I react?

CHAPTER SIX

WE ENTERED THE DRIVEWAY, leading to the gate, which was opened by an old man, dressed in his Sunday best, wearing a blue serge suit, a white shirt and a colorful tie and shiny shoes. His hair was pure white and his face was beaming. I saw no marks of leprosy on him.

"Good morning Sam. How are you?"

"Ise fine, Faddah and you?"

Father Kiely said in his Irish brogue, "The top of the morning, Sam."

"They's waiting for you, Faddah."

He closed the gates behind us and we proceeded up the driveway leading to a two story wooden framed building. It was painted white with green shutters and a wide screened-in veranda ran along the length of both stories. As we parked the car and opened the doors I could hear the savage bark of several dogs.

I hesitated, but Father said, "Don't worry, they are penned up in the day. They won't hurt you. But God forbid you come after dark. You will be torn to bits."

Waiting at the screen door of the lower veranda were two nuns, dressed in a white habit with a starched coronet. Father Kiely introduced me.

"Sergeant," he said, "this is Mother Mary Mark. She belongs to the Superior General's Council."

Mother Mark was beautiful and had a warm smile as she clasped my hand and said, "Welcome, Sergeant. We are so glad to have you."

Then he introduced me to the other nun who was without a doubt, Irish. Her cheeks were red and flushed, her blue eyes dancing.

Father said, "This is my favorite from the old sod, Sister Mary Zita."

"Away with you, Father," she said, in a thick Irish brogue.

She too grasped my hands welcoming me. We entered the large comfortable veranda, protected from the insects by screens. There were ferns and flowers everywhere, sofas and easy chairs. This was the Sisters' recreation room. There was a piano at one end and several instruments.

Mother said, "I would offer you something to drink, Father, but I know that you are anxious to get to the patients for Mass."

In those days you were not allowed to eat or drink before Communion. I was petrified. I looked around but I could not see any patients. Some hundred yards in the distance was another wall and that was the entrance into the Compound.

Mother Mark must have sensed my nervousness for she took my hand and she said, "Everything will be all right, now don't worry. Just come along."

We followed them on a dusty path leading to the Compound. At the gate was a handsome young black man, neatly dressed.

"This is Cornelius," Mother Mark said. "He takes care of things around here and he is our right hand man."

He did not offer his hand nor did I offer mine and I searched for signs of leprosy but except for a few crooked fingers I could see none.

He bowed his head and softly said, "Welcome, Sergeant."

Sister Zita said, "Cornelius keeps control over the Compound."

I could see that it was divided by another wall with the women on one side and the men on the other side.

Sister pointed out a small concrete building and said, "That is the prison."

"Prison?" I said.

She said, "Yes, you must remember that these people are confined and there are problems, sometimes serious, and the local jails will not accept the leprosy patients."

I was learning something every minute. I could see barracks built on cement blocks, not as modern as those at the Base but the same type of structure. Some were dilapidated with the paint peeling while others were newly being built. Father was anxious to get to the Chapel so I did not ask any questions. The Chapel was a wide long building with a slanted roof, and on the top was a Cross. It was badly in need of repair. We climbed the steps and entered the Sacristy. Another nun was there preparing the vestments and she was introduced as Sister Marina. Father must have told them in advance that he was bringing an Army Sergeant for it seemed as if they were expecting me and welcomed me warmly.

I was about to go out into the Church to take my place in the pew when Father said, "You are going to serve my Mass."

I was thunderstruck. I said, "Father, I have never served Mass."

"You haven't?" he said. "Where did you go to school?"

"I went to public schools, Father."

He said, "Oh! Well, you have been to Mass enough to know what the altar boy does. Don't you?"

I said, "Yes, I can do what he does but I don't know the Latin responses."

"Don't worry about that," he said, "I will take care of it."

Now I was more shaken than I was when I went to the Leprosarium. Suppose I drop things or spill things or ring the bell at the wrong time? Well, Father was Commander-in-Chief in this Chapel so I had to obey. After vesting, we rang the bell and entered the altar area. It was beautifully decorated with vases of roses, wild orchids, honeysuckle, hibiscus and other flowers. There were tall candlesticks that were lit and the altar was covered with a beautiful white linen cloth. In 1941, the altar did not face the congregation and Latin was the official language of the Mass. I was shaking like a leaf as I tried to remember every movement of the altar boys. As we knelt at the altar, for the opening prayers of the Mass, I started to mumble my response when Father said, "I'll take it. Don't try."

I was grateful. Most of the time I had my back to the congregation and that was OK by me as I had yet to see the true victims of leprosy. When it was time for the Gospel, I looked out at the congregation. Everyone was dressed in their Sunday best. Many had on straw hats, beautifully decorated and the women had on long white dresses and the men were in black suits. I concentrated looking at their clothes rather than at their bodies.

After the Gospel, Father gave a short homily and turned to me and said, "I have brought with me a Sergeant from the United States Army Base who has just arrived in Jamaica."

The Sisters must have prepared them for they broke out in applause. My face was burning with embarrassment. When it came time to hand Father the cruets of wine and water, I was gripping them so tightly that he had to pull them out of my hand. Then when it came time for me to pour the holy water over his fingers, my hand was shaking so much that I was splattering the water all over the place so he grabbed the cruet and poured water over his own hands. I thought he would be angry but he had a smile on his face. I think he was enjoying my torture. They were all lined up at the altar rail. We were not allowed to touch the host then so I stood next to Father holding the Communion plate and placed it under the chin of the first patient, a little old lady with stumps for hands and a hole in her face where there was once a nose. My hand began to shake again but Father now looked at me sternly as I passed from communicant to communicant. It became more gruesome as many had large swellings on their face, ear lobes almost hanging to their shoulders, their mouths covered with sores. Some had no eyebrows or eyelashes and their fingers were swollen, bandaged and soaked with pus. I had worked in emergency rooms in my hospital days where I saw gunshot and knife wounds, broken bones, lacerations, amputated limbs from car accidents but none affected me as much as what I was seeing. I was beginning to feel faint but I dared not fall down in front of these people who believed an Army Sergeant was a brave man. I kept my face from showing any shock for I knew that I would cause them pain. Mass ended and we returned to the Sacristy. Sister Marina had sensed my nervousness and beckoned me to sit in an armchair as she gave me a cold Coca-Cola and a cookie.

Father Kiely was laughing, not about my reaction to the patients but my ineptitude at serving his Mass but he was kind and he said, "You did well, Sarge."

We had become very close friends by now, so I said, "Yeah, you better go to confession. You are telling a lie."

Then Mother Mary Mark and Sister Zita entered the Sacristy and said they would take me back to the convent for breakfast.

Father said, "You go ahead. I will be along in a little while. I have some things to do here."

As we left the Sacristy to walk back to the convent there were clusters of patients gathered around. They waved and smiled. I had regained my composure by now and I waved back.

When we got back to the convent, Mother and Sister excused themselves and took me to the veranda where another Sister by the name of Sister Mary Germane, brought me a glass of orange juice. When they returned they were in their black habits. They explained to me that the white habit was used when they were in the Compound. They had to change into another white habit for the convent since any clothing worn in the Compound, including shoes, was considered to be contaminated. The exception was that they had to wear their original black habit whenever they left the Leprosarium to go into town. I had a thousand questions, but I thought I would hold them for Father. We chatted for a while. They were anxious to know where I was from and I told them I was from New Jersey. Sister Zita said that she was originally from Ireland but her parents had settled in Staten Island when she joined the Marist. Mother Mark said she was from Boston and was one of the first American Sisters to join the Congregation. She had been elected as a member of the Mother General's Council and had been scheduled to go to France to the Mother House, at Lyon, to serve out her term when war broke out and all travel to Europe was cancelled. Her headquarters was in Bedford, Massachusetts. but they had just taken over management of the Leprosarium, which was under the control of the Jamaican government.

"Before our arrival," Mother said, "civilian officials from the Jamaican government supervised the running of the Leprosarium but they were fearful of the patients and had little control over them. The new Governor General had held the same position in Fiji where our Sisters had one of the most modern leprosy hospitals in Makongai."

Mother Mary Mark praised Sister Zita's handling of the situation for Sister was very shy. She told of the obstacles they faced since the Catholics were in the minority in Jamaica. It was predominantly Anglican since it was under British rule. However, the Governor was adamant and trusted the Sisters to make the necessary changes. There were nine nuns in the original contingent. They arrived a few months before I came to Jamaica. The Sisters found conditions deplorable. The wards were filthy, patients unkempt, bandages unchanged and they lived in fear of one another. Mother said many of them would climb the walls at night and go into Spanish Town where they would be rounded up by the police and brought back to the Compound. Some stole food from the kitchens and sold it. When people knew that the food came from the Leprosarium, there was panic. The local Constabulary, who were fearful of the patients, did not want to patrol inside the Compound. They set up their patrols outside the walls. The Sisters had worked miracles in the short time that they had been there. Dressed in their white habits, many of the patients were fearful of the Sisters and called them "debils" but they soon won over the confidence of all with their loving care. They did not shun them as the previous workers had. They dressed their sores, changed their bandages, and listened to their problems and woes. I was fascinated by what they were telling me when Father Kiely arrived. I had so much to learn but Father was hungry so we were escorted into the small guest dining room next to the Sisters' dining room. Beyond I could see the cookhouse and kitchen that was staffed by two Jamaican women whom I later learned were not patients. The Sisters brought in a large bowl of fresh fruit with platters of eggs, bacon and fried potatoes. There was a coffee pot of delicious Blue Mountain coffee, which Father told me was prized around the world. I picked at my food as I did not have an appetite but Father Kiely dug hungrily into his.

Looking at my plate he said, “You know, Sergeant, if you don’t eat that, the Sisters will have to eat the leftovers.”

I had little knowledge of what Sisters did and believed him, so I gulped down every morsel of food, leaving my plate clean. This seemed to satisfy the Sister who came in and cleared away the dishes.

Father was anxious to get back to May Pen for he had confessions, not only at his Chapel but at the Army Base as well. The Sisters were disappointed but he promised to bring me back during the week.

CHAPTER SEVEN

THEY WAVED GOODBYE AS WE entered his car and passed through the gates onto the road leading to Spanish Town. I loosened my tie. It was not air conditioned, but with the windows open a warm but refreshing breeze blew through the car.

We were silent for awhile and he turned to me and said, "Well?"

I looked at him and I said, "I know now what you meant when you said to me, 'You don't know how lucky you are,' when I griped about conditions at the Base." I sighed, "These people have nowhere to go and if they did no one would accept them. They are virtual prisoners."

"You can say that again," he said.

"The Sisters are better soldiers than we are," I said.

"They too are confined but they are happy that they are there for they have chosen to spend their life taking care of these people."

"It's not easy," Father said. "They have to fight for everything from the Government, especially now that England is at war and supplies are hard to obtain. The Sisters can tell you more about that the next time we visit them."

He cursed under his breath as he swerved to avoid hitting a goat. I was holding on tight to the door of the car.

He laughed and said, "I'm off on Wednesday. I have to go to Kingston and I could drop you off at Spanish Town and pick you up on the way back if you want to go."

"I will have to ask the Captain," I said.

"Leave it to me," he said and I did.

During the next few days I kept looking for signs that I had leprosy but everything seemed to be intact. On Wednesday the hospital staff asked me where I was going. I did not want them to know that I was going to a Leprosarium and create fear, so I said that I was going to Kingston with Father Kiely and left it at that.

Father was late which was unusual for him. I assumed he had some emergency and I was about to go back into the barracks when I saw his old Ford approach the hospital entrance. When I got in he apologized.

He said, "Sorry I am late but Virginette had problems with her children."

I smiled. I had met Virginette. She was a light skinned Jamaican of about 30 years of age and served as Father's housekeeper. She lived in a little hut behind the rectory with her three children. Like a large number of Jamaican women she had no husband. Thus the name Virginette always brought smiles to my face. Father was dressed in his usual outfit of a white linen suit, a black vest and a white starched collar that most priests on the island wore. He was of medium build in his early 40's with black straight hair tinged with gray. His face was like a map of Ireland and his eyes were always twinkling. He had been in Jamaica for seven years and his hometown was Lynn, Massachusetts.

We passed through the gate jammed with the usual crowd of Jamaicans, babbling and yelling, "We want the job. Me a good carpenter."

The M.P.'s were posting the available jobs for the day. Across the road at the edge of the shantytown were women and children laying out their straw mats with produce of bananas, coconuts, pineapples, mangoes and other goods for sale. Others were selling beautiful straw hats. Still others had kitchen utensils and almost anything that they could get their hands on to sell and make a few shillings. They were poorly dressed and the children looked ragged. My heart went out to them but there were too many to handle for if you gave to one, you would be surrounded. You would have to ignore others and that was hard for me to do. I just steeled myself whenever I went by.

"Was Virginette sick?" I asked.

"No, she had trouble finding one of her little ones. I can't leave unless she is there for she takes care of the office as well as the house."

I smiled again as I knew the house was tiny, consisting of a bedroom, a guest room, a small dining room and a cramped office with a battered old desk. The cooking was done as in most places, outside on an open fire covered by a grill. The smell of burnt wood was always mingled in with the other smells, like roasting chickens, goats and pigs. After a period of time you became used to the smells and you were seldom aware of them. But somehow you never forget the smell of the burnt wood fires. Even today they remind me of Jamaica. It wasn't long before we turned onto the Spanish Town road. It was comparatively empty for it was Wednesday morning and most of the traffic that clogged the roads happened on Friday evening as the carts and wagons carried their produce into Kingston for Saturday market. The speed limit was 25 miles per hour, which you seldom reached since there were always goats crossing the road and carts being drawn by the mules, jackasses and oxen. I had gotten used to the sight of carts piled high with produce being driven by a Jamaican sitting on a seat cracking a whip while behind walked the women with their heads bowed with the weight of bundles that they carried on their head. The women had a tough life in Jamaica. In our many talks during the weeks that followed my arrival in Jamaica, I had asked Father why they did not marry. His answer, he said simply, was pride. They must have the proper clothing, a good dress and shoes before they were walked down the aisle and most men refused to take on the burden of caring for a family. It is the women who are the backbone of family life, Father told me. In many cases once the young boy reached their teens the father would claim them. They would be forced to work by their father's side in the cane fields and factories. The father would take whatever they were paid and give them just a small amount to live on. That is why many men are not happy when their partners give birth to females.

I leaned back in my seat and enjoyed the soft breeze blowing in the window gazing out at the beautiful scenery. We passed by the open road with the waving green fields of sugarcane and bananas. I had yet to be given a pass into Kingston so I could explore, but my trips to May Pen did give me an inkling as to life in a small Jamaican town. I had told Father of my purchase of the book on the history of Jamaica during our stop in Spanish Town.

He turned to me and said, "How are you doing with the history of Jamaica?"

"I haven't gotten very far, Father. We have been so busy. First setting up the old hospital. Then moving into the new one. I haven't had any time to do any reading but I will get to it."

"You will find it fascinating," Father said. "It will make your time here more meaningful if you know the people, their history and their customs. It will give you a better understanding of what life is like for these poor people." He honked his horn as two goats stood defiantly in the middle of the road. We stopped and waited until they made up their minds.

As he started up again, I said, "You know the natives are making a fortune if any of their animals are hit on the road by Army trucks. The Government will pay them handsomely for their loss, which is much more than the animals are worth but it keeps peace. I think some of them drive the goats onto the road hoping that they will be killed."

"Well," he said, "you are beginning to understand the mind of the Jamaican. They may seem to be illiterate but they are smart in the ways of the world. They have so little money yet they will do anything to obtain a few pence. Stealing is rampant and they see nothing wrong with it. For some of them it is the only way they can survive."

"It must be difficult in confession to make decisions when there is so much immorality," I said.

"When you study the history, Sergeant, you will understand them better. I don't call what most of them do immoral but amoral. They lack the background necessary to make moral decisions. That's the job of the Missionary. Missionaries are a special breed. They are trained to face adversity."

"Do you ever miss being in a wealthy parish with the collection being enough to meet the expenses of building schools and making improvements?"

"Stop it," he said. "You sound like the devil tempting me." Then he laughed. "I would never have become a Missionary if I wanted that. Jamaica has many amenities, as I am sure that you are finding out. You are lucky. You could have been stuck in a worse place than this."

He was quiet for a moment, "Enjoy your days," he said. "You don't know what is in store for you in the future."

I thought of the daily bulletins we were given at the Base about the progress of the war in Europe.

"Do you think that we will be in the war, Father?"

"We are in the war, Sergeant. You are in Jamaica."

I then remembered that Jamaica was a British Colony.

"The only thing war-like," Father said, "is the lack of supplies and the restrictions on travel. The unemployment is due to the lack of tourists. You know we depended on them, especially the wealthy and royalty from Europe. As you study the history you will find that although the English have been here for almost 300 years they never really considered Jamaica as their permanent home. Their roots are still in England. They send their children to school there and spend most of their vacation and free time in their mother country. They too have been restricted in travel. Much of the export of bananas, sugar, rum and other Jamaican goods no longer can be shipped as much of the cargo has been sunk by U-Boats." He swatted at a mosquito on his forehead.

He continued, "We are now starting to trade with the United States more than we ever did before. But we don't know how long that will last. That is why you see hundreds of Jamaicans rushing to get jobs at the Army Base. Now that the Base is finished they have lost their job opportunity there as well."

"Have there been any sightings of U-Boats along the coast of Jamaica?" I asked.

"Yes, there have been many. That is why the British and Jamaican forces, as well as the Canadians and Australians are posted in several locations at various coastal towns on the island. There is some fear that they will send Commandos ashore. But so far nothing has happened. Now with the Army and Navy airfield at Fort Simonds, there might be reason for them to send such a force ashore."

"Things don't look so good for England, do they?" I said.

He took out his cigarette, put it in his mouth, lit a match and took a deep puff. He looked at me and said, "I know, I know, don't say anything."

"Do you think that America will be drawn into the war, Father?"

"It's inevitable," he said "and I think that it can come at any time with the fall of France and the bombardment of England, they are going to need our help."

I shifted in my seat. "You know, Father, I will confide to you that as a draftee I was not supposed to be sent overseas." I explained to him about the Medic I replaced. "I'm lucky for I am sure that with my medical background if war broke out, I would have been sent to the front lines."

"God works in strange ways," Father said. "I don't believe in coincidence. There is a divine plan. The roads we are supposed to travel are pretty much mapped out for us but the gift of free will determines whether we take the roads or a detour. It is up to us."

I was silent for a while. I glanced out the window and saw a sign, Spanish Town, ten miles. The conversation had been so interesting that time just flew by.

"Do they know who first inhabited the island?" I asked.

"It is believed that hundreds of years ago the islands were inhabited by Indian tribes. Probably they came here from the islands such as Barbados. Then came the Spaniards followed by the slaves from all parts of Africa. With the Spaniards came other foreigners - Jews from Portugal, Syrians from the Middle East, and Asians from the Far East. Then you must remember that Columbus landed in Jamaica. When the English arrived many of the foreigners were driven out for a time. Many slaves who were fierce fighters fled into the hills of Jamaica, setting up their own government. They are called Maroons and they pretty much govern themselves. With the English came many traders. Many came from British Colonies such as India as well as the Scottish and the Irish. The Puritans from America arrived but they could not stand the decadence of the natives and they soon left. There was much intermingling so that the races were mixed which is what you see today."

I stretched out my legs and noticed that the cigarette was almost to his fingertips and he put it out in the ashtray.

A Missionary, I thought, wastes nothing. We were driving directly into the sun so I put down my visor.

Father was wearing sunglasses and he said to me, "Where are your sunglasses?"

"I don't have any."

"Well, you better get some. You are going to need them here."

I had so many more questions to ask him but I thought that I would wait for the return trip for I was sure that I was tiring him out. I put my hand out of the window to catch a breeze and it was not long before we came to a clump of trees and thick foliage. We were nearing the Rio Cobre River. I gazed wistfully at the blue green waters below, wishing I could take off my clothes and jump in. Not long after we crossed the bridge, we came to the crossroads. To the left was Spanish Town and to the right the Leprosarium. As we pulled up to the gate, Simmons, the old man I had met when we visited last week, came out from the gatehouse and approached the car. Father said he would leave me there and would pick me up at about two-thirty in the afternoon for the ride home and told Simmons that I was expected.

"Welcome, Sergeant," he said, with a mixture of Jamaican and British. It sounded like Sir John.

He said, "Mother is waiting in the convent."

I tipped him a few shillings and he beamed. As I approached the screened in porch of the convent I heard the dogs barking but I knew that they were locked up in their kennels.

CHAPTER EIGHT

MOTHER GREETED ME WARMLY AND ushered me to a cushioned white wicker chair on the patio. On the table beside me was a pitcher of ice-cold lemonade with bits of lime floating and alongside an inevitable plate of cookies covered with a napkin to prevent the insects from eating their fill. She sat down beside me and poured lemonade into a tall glass. I noticed that she did not have any herself. It was now eleven a.m. and several of the Sisters could be seen walking back toward the convent from the Compound. She said it is noontime and we have to eat in shifts, as we must leave some of the Sisters in the Compound at all times. The Sisters waved as they passed in front of us and went into a side door. Mother said they were going into a changing room as they change their habits and their shoes each time they left the Compound and entered the convent. They had to change again to go back to the Compound. She said the Sisters would now have prayers in the chapel and at eleven-thirty would have lunch. They would then return to the Compound to relieve the Sisters who were now serving the meals to the patients.

"We will give them time to clean up." Mother said. "So we can rest a while. Perhaps you have some questions that you would like to ask me before we go over to the Compound?"

"Since my last visit, Mother, my head has been swimming with questions that I can't wait to have answered."

"I'm sure that you would like to know if you can catch leprosy. There are so many false ideas and rumors. Fear is one of the reasons that so few of the patients' families or relatives come to visit them. There are other curious seekers who come for a few minutes and never return, so I am happy to see that you have come back."

"I must confess," I said, reddening slightly, "that Father Kiely has a lot to do with it."

She laughed, "He certainly is a persuasive man. I wish he were our Chaplain, for he could do a lot for us with the Government. Let me assure you that it is almost impossible for you to catch leprosy. The Sisters have been caring for victims of leprosy for many years in our Missions in the South Pacific and we have had only one case of a Sister coming down with the disease."

"That is a relief," I said.

"I'm sure that you are acquainted with the Gospels," Mother said.

"I know that at the time of Christ leprosy was prevalent and He did not fear touching them even though they were declared as unclean. They had to be driven away from their families and homes to live in caves and other isolated places." Mother swatted at a pesky mosquito that was buzzing around. "From what I know it doesn't seem like there has been very much progress since Biblical times in the treatment of leprosy," I said.

"You are right. We still treat those who have leprosy like criminals. Even in the United States if you are diagnosed with leprosy you are torn from your family, put on a freight car that is headed for Carville, Louisiana, which is run by the United States Government."

I sipped some of the lemonade and put the glass down on the table.

"Are you telling me, Mother, that there are leprosy patients in the United States? I didn't know that."

"Not many people do. They keep it quiet. Some commit suicide before they are taken to Carville."

"Man's inhumanity to man," I said.

"Once they are admitted to Carville the Government does everything to make life as comfortable as possible. The good Sisters give them a lot of loving care."

"There are Sisters there? I thought you said that it was run by the United States Government," I said.

"The Daughters of Charity have been caring for the victims of leprosy for many years and before the leprosy hospital was established in Carville, they took care of the leprosy patients in New Orleans in a small isolated building. At first it was kept very secret that they would be going to Carville. The Government had purchased an old dilapidated mansion along the banks of the Mississippi. Much work had to be done. So they renovated the slave quarters to house both the first patients and the Sisters." Mother fingered her rosary.

"How awful," I said. "They were brave women."

Mother nodded her head.

"That they were. They were following in the footsteps of Christ."

"What happened after they arrived there?" I asked.

"They left after midnight from New Orleans on a barge so that they would not be noticed. When they arrived at Carville they were taken to the slave quarters, which had been scrubbed and whitewashed by some of the Sisters who had gone there in advance. The Sisters lived in the same type of quarters as the patients. They had to contend with mosquitoes and many insects. Rats ran all over the place since the grounds had been neglected. Moss covered most of the beautiful trees and were good hiding places for snakes."

I shuddered. "Are there snakes in Jamaica?" I asked Mother.

"No, not many. Most of them have been eradicated but occasionally someone will see a snake. The Jamaican government had introduced the mongoose, a vicious little ferret like animal from India, which was the snake's deadly enemy. Soon most of the snake population was wiped out. With few snakes for the mongoose they turned to chickens and small animals. The mongoose are now a problem here but they do not go after humans unless you corner them."

"I often read that the tropics were like paradise," I laughed.

"The snakes in paradise weren't deadly," Mother said.

"We all know the story of Adam and Eve." She smiled and looked at her watch.

"Oh, my," she said. "The Sisters will be coming for prayers and lunch. What time did Father Kiely say he would pick you up?"

"He said about two-thirty."

I turned to look outside and saw three nuns in white approaching the Convent from the Compound.

I said, "You told me, Mother, that they have to change their clothing. Is leprosy transmitted through clothing?"

Mother said, "We are not sure. It is not positive as to how leprosy is transmitted but we take all the precautions that we can."

"What about me when I visit the Compound?" I asked.

She patted my hand. "Not to worry, Sergeant. Visitors are given a white gown to put on over their clothing when they visit the Compound. We had better be going as the Sisters will be serving lunch to the patients shortly."

She rose from her chair and I took a last sip of the lemonade, a bite of the cookie to strengthen myself as I rose to follow her. As we left, the three nuns were entering the back door. We started toward the Compound. I asked Mother how many nuns there were and she told me that there were nine and that this was the only Mission they had in the Americas as they were founded to serve the peoples of the South Pacific. Since many of the Islands of the South Pacific belonged to England, the state of war existed and all communication and transportation was cut off. We had reached the gates of the Compound and Cornelius, whom I had met on my first visit, opened the gates for us. He was a young man dressed as usual in his black trousers, a white shirt and a dark tie. Except for his hands, I saw no sign of leprosy.

Mother said, "You know Cornelius, don't you, Sergeant?"

"Yes, hello Cornelius, it is good to see you again." I held out my hand but he did not take it.

"You are most welcome, Sergeant." Again it sounded as though he had said, Sir John.

Mother took me first to the office that was located in a building that resembled a cottage. As we entered the office, a Sister who Mother introduced to me as Sister Mary Germaine, greeted us. She was a very thin nun who kept her eyes downward and did not look directly at me. Welcoming me, she turned and went about her tasks. Later Mother told me that she was one of the most dedicated Sisters that she had ever known. When she was not working she was constantly at prayer. She had the unenviable task of cleaning the running sores, many of which were infected. Bandages could not be taped on because of the sensitive skin. The bandage would be held in place by a roll of cloth usually made from linen sheets, cut into long strips.

"Bandages," Mother said, "were expensive so Sister would take the pus-stained cloths, boil them and hang them out to dry so that they could be used over again."

I cringed at the thought of touching the pus-stained bandages. Mother handed me a long white gown to put on over my uniform. She told me that they did not wear masks, which the former government employees would wear. The mask would cause a wide chasm between the patients and the worker. The patients, she had also told me, had been warned that when they sneezed or coughed, to turn their heads or cover their mouths. I noticed a long table in one room with several microscopes with stacks of slides and chemicals.

Mother said, "This was the laboratory where they would study the slides and count the bacilli. In another room the shelves were lined with bottles of different kinds of medicines. Just beyond was another room with a long wooden table, which was used for operations, usually amputations. The surgeon from Spanish Town would visit every other day to take care of the more serious cases."

When I looked at the equipment and furnishings, and compared them to the glistening new equipment of the Base Hospital, I realized even more the sacrifices that these women were making. I felt guilty that we had so much and they had so little. A thought popped into my mind. We threw away so much that could still be used. I wondered if I could bring some of that here. Mother took me to the women's Compound after I put on the long white gown similar to what we used in our operating rooms. She explained that a wall between the men and women's Compound was necessary to maintain discipline. The patients were sexually active and there was a high incidence of venereal disease, especially syphilis. In addition any child born had to be removed almost immediately for fear that the child would contract leprosy through direct skin-to-skin contact.

"Where do the children go, Mother?" I asked.

"We have a nursery and a pediatric department in another building. They are separated from the other patients. The mother can see the baby but cannot touch him."

I shook my head as I thought of the poor mother not being able to touch her baby.

"In some other cases," Mother said, "members of the family who do not have leprosy will come and take the baby to raise them. But not too many families will even visit here."

As we entered the women's Compound I saw that many barracks were on cement blocks. These were the dormitories, which I discovered held about 10 or 12 beds. The whole space was open with no partions to allow privacy. In oblong concrete buildings located between the dormitories were the latrines and showers. I noticed that some of the dormitories were old and dilapidated while others had been newly built and brightly painted. Mother explained to me that when the nuns arrived the living conditions were deplorable.

"Sister Mary Zita is a dynamo and a politician," she laughed. "Only the Governor approved of bringing us here to work. Most other officials objected, as they were afraid that the nuns would convert all of the patients to Catholicism. It was difficult going at first to get the available funds to make improvements."

We were standing under a large flowering tree of poinciana. Some women stood at a distance watching us. Any newcomer was of great interest to them.

Mother went on, "The first thing that Sister did was to renovate the Seventh Day Adventist, the Anglican and the Baptist Chapels. When you attended Mass last week I am sure that you were aware that our own Chapel needed much work. Sister Zita knew that if she had renovated the Catholic Chapel first, they would be upset. When we need new equipment they require first that we show them the old equipment before they will authorize the purchase. Sister Zita told them that she would follow their instructions but could not guarantee that the old equipment that she would bring them would be free of the leprosy bacillus. So that order was rescinded immediately," she said, smilingly.

"When I first met Sister Zita, I thought that she was shy." I said.

"Sister cannot stand any attention being paid to her. She has great humility and reddens whenever anyone praises her but beneath her exterior is a will of iron. That was one of the reasons why she was elected Superior," Mother replied. We started to walk toward one of the dormitories.

Mother said, "We won't have time to visit all of the dormitories but if you see one, most of the others are similar."

We climbed a few wooden steps and entered the open doorway. The beds were all neatly made and covered with colorful red bedspreads. At each bedside table there was a vase of flowers. Some held photographs but most were bare except for the flowers. Mother explained that stealing was rampant, even among the patients. They kept most of their belongings in a battered suitcase under the bed. She told me that it was sad but an amusing sight to see some of them come to Mass with their suitcase on their head, fearful of leaving it at their bedside. They had little of worth that anyone could steal, as they did not possess any coins or paper money. Everything that they bought in the patients' store, from earning money and doing chores, was all kept in a ledger. Each month the Government would give a small stipend to each patient with which they could buy soap, powder and trinkets, dominoes, checkers, tobacco and the like. When they made a purchase it would be deducted from their account. Since they were only given the equivalent of $1.00 a week, there was not much that they could purchase. The women loved to embroider and the Sisters would purchase the material with gifts that they had received from the States. I met many of the women who were neatly dressed. The Sisters must have told them that I would visit. They were all friendly but shy. Many had no fingers and no toes. I could detect the difference between those with lepromatous and those with the neural type of leprosy and some had both. It was difficult to disguise the odor of rotting flesh but I made every physical effort to hide any reaction that would have caused them pain. Mother did not disapprove of me holding out my hand for a handshake. She told me that I would scrub with soap and disinfectant before I would return to the Convent. At first it took a great deal of nerve on my part to offer my hand but when I saw how grateful many of them were to feel the touch of another human being, especially one who did not have the disease, it was easy. In the months and years to come I would get to know them all by name and the personality of each one of them. They were human after all with their own temperament, likes and dislikes.

On the men's side some of them were bold and forward, while others were defiant and would not come forward to greet me. Some had hostile stares. It was almost two o'clock when we returned to the Convent. I had removed my gown in the office and Sister gave me green liquid soap, which we used in the operating rooms, to scrub my hands. When we returned to the Convent Sister Zita was there awaiting our arrival and took me to the small guest dining room where they had prepared tasty chicken sandwiches and hot tea. I had just about finished when I heard the honking of a horn. Father Kiely was there. The Sisters invited him in for refreshments but he refused saying that he had to get back to May Pen. I bid Sister Zita farewell and I told them that they had not seen the last of me.

CHAPTER NINE

I HOPPED INTO THE CAR BESIDE Father Kiely and we took off. As I settled back in the seat I noticed that he had taken his coat off. He had rolled up the sleeves of his white shirt and I noticed that his vest was stained with ashes and food stains. He did not seem to be in a good mood.

It was not until we turned onto the Spanish Town road that he turned to me and said, "Well, how did your day go?"

"Don't worry about my day," I said. "What about yours? You don't look happy."

He smiled and said, "I'm sorry that I am so grumpy. I had some problems with the Bishop."

I kept silent figuring that it would be up to him to tell me. I would not pry.

"By now you know that I have a short Irish temper and it is so difficult to get supplies that I lose patience, but then I have to remember that the Bishop has his problems too."

He took out the pack of cigarettes from his shirt pocket and removed the last cigarette. He looked at the pack in disgust and crumpled it.

"This will have to last until I get home."

I looked out the window and said softly but loud enough for him to hear me, "Good."

"You are treading on my toes," he said sharply. I didn't reply. "Well, how did things go?"

I told him about everything that had happened to me since he left.

"Have you suddenly realized how good you have it compared to these poor people?" he said.

I removed my cap and wiped my brow, as it was very warm. "I have got to do something for them, Father."

He looked at me sharply and said, "What do you mean? Do something for them?"

"Well, for one thing Christmas is coming and I know that I could get the guys to chip in to buy them some presents for Christmas and our Base orchestra is good and I am sure that they would be willing to put on a show for them."

He looked at me for a few moments and then said, "God works His ways."

I turned to look at him and said, "What do you mean, Father?"

"Well, it seems that He has planted a seed. He is telling you that there are people that need you and you can use your talents to help them."

I grinned and said, "Then you approve of the idea?"

"Well, you have your Commander to ask first. You will need permission."

"I think that I can handle that. Captain Holland and I seem to get along. I'm sure that he will help." I paused. "Maybe he will even be able to give me some medical supplies that the poor Sisters need desperately and if he doesn't, well."

"Well, what?" Father said sharply. "I think I know what's in your mind. Don't be committing thievery in the name of charity."

I turned to look at him, "Father," I said, "whatever would give you a thought that I would steal?" He gave a loud laugh.

"I have come up against characters like you all of my life. They think that God would approve if they became a modern Robin Hood, robbing from the rich to give to the poor." He puffed on his cigarette. "If you do such a thing and get caught, don't count on me to get you out of the brig."

"You don't have to worry, Father. Every time I do something wrong I more than pay for it with a guilty conscience. I take after my Mother."

I told him of the time when my Mother was a little girl. She took a dollar from her mother's pocketbook. A dollar in those days was a fortune and she went downtown to buy all kinds of goodies for the poor children in the neighborhood. When her Mother discovered that the dollar was missing, she lined up all of her children and asked them if they took the dollar. When she came to my Mother she didn't have to answer. She threw up. Father grabbed at his coat lying on the seat next to him and put it over his lap. I had a hearty laugh.

"Don't worry, Father," I said. "I am not going to throw up on your coat. I haven't done anything wrong yet."

"And don't even think about it," he replied.

After a few moments of driving in silence, he said, "I thought of all that we were talking about on the way in. About the history of the Island, etc."

"Father, I won't ask any more questions for a while. Between our conversations this morning and all that Mother Mary Mark told me about the history of leprosy, my mind seems to be so full of information. I feel like it is going to burst."

"That's good," he said. "I have a lot on my mind for the weekend. I have so much to do."

"Like what?" I asked.

"You think that you are busy. I get up earlier than you. I say at least an hour of prayers before my breakfast. Then I have to worry about you guys on the Base with confession and Masses, try to solve family squabbles, and I also have to prepare my van to visit several villages to celebrate Mass, and before I can shut my eyes at night there are more prayers."

"Enough already, Father. You have convinced me. My day is nothing compared to yours."

We had reached the outskirts of the Base as we slowed down behind the line of jeeps and trucks, entering the gates. I noticed in the large crowd of beggars along the side of the road, the same beautiful little girl dressed in ragged clothes hunched over a straw basket of fruit, which she was selling.

Her face had haunted me and I turned to Father and said, "Look at that poor little girl. She looks so sad."

Father glanced to where I was pointing and said, "Oh, yes. That's Grace. She and her Granny, once in a while, do come to Mass. They walk all the way from here to May Pen."

Grace, I thought. What a beautiful name and I thought of our Blessed Mother. Hail Mary full of grace. In the weeks to come I would get to know that little girl and her Granny and the pitiful life that she had led. Father left me off at my barracks, inside the Base. I thanked him and he said that he would see me at Mass on Sunday at the Base Chapel. What a day this has been, I thought, as I went to my bunk. I plopped down and a kaleidoscope of images and thoughts raced through my mind of the eventful day that I had just spent, thinking of others rather than myself. I wasted no time in discussing the project for the Leprosarium with my close buddies and with Captain Holland. They were excited about the idea and we started to make plans.

CHAPTER TEN

THE MEMBERS OF THE BASE ORCHESTRA were eager to perform. I called Mother Mary Mark. The telephone communications on the island were difficult as they often broke down but I finally got through. She seemed to be enthusiastic about the idea and when I mentioned that we would buy gifts of clothing for each of the patients, she thought that it would be very difficult to do this. She suggested that we give gifts such as soap to all of the women, dolls and toys to the children and shaving equipment and dominoes for the men. I told her that would be easy for us to obtain at the Post Exchange. I asked her when would be the best time to come. She suggested that we come on Boxing Day, the day after Christmas. This is the day that there is exchanging of gifts throughout the British Empire and Jamaica is part of the Empire. I told her that I would keep her in touch with our plans.

We eagerly looked forward to the Mail Call when we would get letters from home. Mom wrote regularly and I devoured every word of her letters. I wrote her about my visit to the Leprosarium and told her what we had planned to do for Christmas. Just like my Mom to take on the project! She would contact all of our relatives and friends who would be eager to help. I wrote right back and told her that would be great but how would they get the gifts to Jamaica? In her next letter she told me to figure it out and she would just get the gifts.

Once again I went to Captain Holland who asked the Base Commander, Colonel Ewing. He was sympathetic to the idea and said he would talk to the Commanding Officer of the Air Base and see what could be done. He called me into his office just two days later. It was the first time that I had met personally with him and I was truly frightened. I made sure that my shoes were highly polished as well as my belt buckle. I arrived at the Headquarters, ahead of the time of the appointment so that I would not be late. The outer office contained many desks. It was a beehive of activity with both Army personnel and civilian Jamaicans who served as part of the Colonel's staff. There was a neatly dressed light skinned Jamaican woman with white hair seated behind the information desk. She also operated a small switchboard. When she asked if she could help me I told her that I was Staff Sergeant Crouch who had an appointment to see Colonel Ewing. She pointed to a desk in the middle of the room and said that I should report to Master Sergeant McGuire. I approached his desk. He was a good looking young man in his early twenties with dark black hair, light blue eyes and a winning smile. As soon as he spoke I knew that he was from New England.

He told me to sit in the chair at the side of his desk and said, "Your name has been mentioned often here in the last few days. You are known as the Leper Colony Sergeant." I could feel my face reddening.

He said, "I understand that you want to help them and I would like to help as well. If there is anything that I can do just let me know. One of my duties is to provide transportation as I am in charge of the Motor Pool."

That interested me. This would be a good guy to know, I thought. Finally his phone rang and he said, "Yes, Sir."

Then he turned to me and said, "Go through that door. The Colonel will see you."

My heart was beating like a hammer. I opened the door and entered a neat office. Seated behind the lone desk was an

Army Captain. I approached the desk, stood at attention and saluted smartly and he returned my salute. He pointed to a row of three chairs and told me to be seated and the Colonel would see me shortly. Soon two other officers entered. I stood and saluted them. They returned the salute and sat in the chairs alongside me. They too had an appointment with the Colonel.

Soon a buzzer sounded on the Captain's desk and he pointed to me and said, "The Colonel will see you now, Sergeant." He stood up and opened the door and announced me, "Colonel Ewing, this is Sergeant Crouch."

I stood in front of his desk and saluted smartly. The Colonel was a tall, slim, handsome man with white hair and a ruddy complexion.

He saluted me in return and said, "At ease, Sergeant. Have a seat there. Relax. I have been informed that you have visited the Spanish Town Leper Colony with Father Kiely."

"Yes, Sir."

He folded his hands together and leaned on the desk.

"I am happy to see our soldiers becoming involved in humanitarian projects for these poor people. So I applaud your interest." I shifted uneasily in my chair. He went on, "It is my understanding that you wish to take some of the troops as well as the Base orchestra to the Leper Colony and to bring Christmas treats and entertainment for the patients. Is that so?"

"Yes, Sir." I was hoping that I could get permission to do that." I could feel the sweat trickling down my back.

"Well," he said, "I heartily approve as long as you submit your plans to me so that we will not either infringe on the rights of the Jamaicans or deviate from Army rules and regulations. Do you understand that, Sergeant?"

"Yes, Sir," I said. "I understand it very well."

"Well, you discuss whatever you plan with Sergeant McGuire and work through him." He stood up. I stood up nervously. He shook my hand and said, "I congratulate you on your interest, Sergeant. I am not a Catholic myself but I appreciate the work that Father Kiely is doing to build up the morale of the troops. Keep in touch," he said.

I saluted smartly and he returned the salute. I pivoted on my heels and marched out of his office. When the door closed behind me I gave a sigh of relief and the Captain seated at his desk grinned. I left his office and went over to Sergeant McGuire.

"How did it go?" he said.

"The Colonel said that if I need anything to discuss it with you and then you would report to him."

McGuire grinned. "I don't think that you will have any trouble getting what you want. The Colonel is a pushover for anything that will build up the morale of the men."

He took a pen and a piece of paper and jotted down a number. He told me that when I wanted to see him to just call the number or if you see me in the NCO Club don't hesitate to talk to me.

"I will, Sergeant. Thanks for everything."

I left the building. That was the beginning of a strong friendship and he was my conduit to the Brass.

Father Kiely gave permission to take up a collection after the Masses on Sunday in the Catholic Chapel. I left it to the non-catholics to speak to their ministers. After Mass the next Sunday, the special collection basket contained almost $300.00. This was amazing since most of the men on the Base were regular Army. I was among only a handful of draftees and they did not have very much money. McGuire saw me after Mass.

"Good news," he said.

"The Commander of the Air Base said that he would make every effort to try to get the gifts that your Mother is collecting to Jamaica before Christmas. Since she lives near Fort Dix it would be easier for your Mother to bring the box of gifts over there, clearly labeled for Fort Simonds, Jamaica." He gave me a slip of paper. "Tell her to bring them to the Quartermaster Building and ask for Sergeant O'Rourke. He will take it from there."

I wrote Mom and told her how to pack the boxes so that they would be sturdy and withstand a lot of handling and to try not to include anything breakable. In her next letter she gave me a list of what they were going to send. There was soap, tooth brushes, toothpaste, hair brushes, combs, costume jewelry, rag dolls, spinning tops, jacks, skipping rope and games along with checkers, dominoes and parcheesi, clay pipes, bags of hard candy, popcorn, pencils, composition pads and the like. She also informed me that there would be a package for each nun. Good old Mom, I thought. She wasted no time and I am sure that she depleted her cookie jar where she kept spare money for special treats or special occasions.

When Thanksgiving came the Colonel, knowing that we would be homesick at times such as these, made sure that we would celebrate Thanksgiving with as much tradition as possible. The morning of Thanksgiving we carried out our usual duties. There were only three patients in the hospital. The Catholics went to the Chapel for Mass, the others to their individual churches for services. Father Kiely said Mass and then we all assembled in front of the Base Headquarters. A small stage was erected on which sat members of the Base Command and Colonel Ewing. The band played "America the Beautiful." We were told to stand at ease. Then Colonel Ewing approached the microphone and read the Thanksgiving Proclamation from President Roosevelt. This was followed by his own words of "Greeting" informing us that he knew that we were all probably homesick but everything had been done to make this day as much like home as possible. When he had finished he bade us all to have a Happy Thanksgiving. We applauded and broke ranks to go to the main Mess

Hall. On this occasion both officers and enlisted men sat together instead of in separate parts of the dining hall. At each plate, to my pleasant surprise, was a chocolate turkey and a printed menu, the cover of which was a drawing of the Command Headquarters with an American flag. Inside was a short prayer of welcome from the Commanding Officer and the menu of the day. It started with a puree of pumpkin soup and compote of fresh Jamaican fruit, bananas, oranges, pineapple, mango and papaya. Next came the main course, roast turkey with stuffing, candied sweet potatoes, mashed potatoes and gravy, string beans, peas and carrots and cranberry sauce and for dessert there was both mince and pumpkin pie. We passed through the food line and came back with heaping plates. There was much laughter and talking. As I ate my dinner my thoughts sped back to my home in New Brunswick where I knew that they were all around the groaning Thanksgiving table. My Mom loved the holidays. She went all out but I was certain that this one was not like the past for one of her boys was missing. After the meal we were given a free day to do whatever we wished. I spent most of the afternoon on my bunk reading the material that Mother Mary Mark had given me on the history of Jamaica and a book on the life of Father Damien. It was fascinating reading and the time flew by quickly. For supper we had cold turkey sandwiches and potato chips. As it grew dark we assembled in the open-air theatre to watch an old movie called, "Gold Diggers." It was pure escapism. After the movie I went to the Non-Commissioned Officers Club. This was reserved for Corporals and Sergeants. Beer was not my forte so I settled for a glass of coke with a dash of Jamaican rum and sought out my friend, Sergeant McGuire. He asked me how plans were going for our Christmas treat for the people in Spanish Town. I told him everything was going fine except I was worried.

"What are you worried about?" he asked.

"Well, I wonder if all of the gifts my Mother has packed will arrive in time," I answered, taking a sip of my drink.

"Don't worry so. If the Commander said that he would get it here it will be here."

His words came to fruition, for two days later I received a call from him that several large wooden crates had arrived and he was arranging for a truck to deliver them to the Hospital. I panicked and thought, where would I put them? Captain Holland came to my rescue again as there was an empty ward and he said that we could store them there until Boxing Day.

The face of Grace had haunted me ever since I saw her that day when I was with Father Kiely after we returned from the Leprosarium. Since she and her Granny attended Mass I gave Father some money to purchase a dress for Granny and a white embroidered dress for Grace. He had spoken to one of the merchants in May Pen who had fulfilled the request. He promised that he would present it to them if he saw them during the Christmas season. Since the area across from the Base was off limits to Army personnel I knew that it would be impossible for me to present it to them myself. In addition, if I was seen presenting them gifts, I would have been mobbed by all of the people living there, begging for gifts. They would resent Grace and her Granny and they would be harmed.

CHAPTER ELEVEN

ON FRIDAY, DECEMBER 5, 1941, I was given a weekend pass to Kingston. It was the first opportunity I had had to visit the Capital since we entered the harbor in August. I had not left the Base since my arrival except for my two trips to Spanish Town. The USO had purchased a choice piece of land in the suburb of Kingston known as Half Way Tree. They had built a canteen and a dormitory for servicemen on leave. Nearby was also the Holy Cross Cathedral, the Headquarters of the Jesuits and St. George College, an educational institution. Most of the middle class Jamaicans lived in the area with neat cottages and large homes, surrounded by gardens and protective fences. There were stores and shops of every description and a new large indoor theatre that just had been completed. It was the first air-conditioned theatre and was named the Caribe. Many nightclubs and bars catering to the middle and upper classes were scattered about.

The island was controlled by Great Britain. A class system depended on the color of the skin. The lighter the skin the more opportunity to be better educated. They held better paying jobs as secretaries, businessmen and professionals. Most of the light skinned Jamaicans could trace back through their history and find that they are the result of the intermingling of races in the past, which they kept secret. The English maintained their upper class distinction and with their social ladder kept their distance from the natives.

They held the highest level of power and their children attended schools in England. Many of the more wealthy Jamaicans, Asians, Europeans and those who came from the Middle East, as well as Americans who settled on the island, sent their children to the private schools. The English did provide many public schools for the lower classes where they learned reading, writing and skills to prepare them for work as domestics, tradesmen and in agriculture. Not every Jamaican mother could send her children to school for she insisted that they be properly dressed. She could not afford it and in addition, many children were needed to work in the plantations, farms and the markets.

Nearly every middle and upper class family had servants. Maids, gardeners, cook and wash women. Those who worked on the inside of the house considered themselves superior to those who worked on the outside. They were not known to be industrious. Their pay was small with no incentive for promotion, raises or recognition. It took more than one maid to clean a small cottage and several in the pantry to prepare the meals. Most of the shopping for food was left to the head cook who took her job seriously and wielded great power over the other servants. The business and work hours of the Jamaican was regulated by the temperature since there was no air conditioning at the time in offices, shops, restaurants or even in hotels. Ceiling fans were everywhere. Many businesses closed for several hours from noon to three o'clock, the hottest time of the day. From five to seven was time for High Tea or cocktails and the evening meal was seldom served before eight o'clock. Most domestics worked twelve hours a day, six or seven days a week. In order to ensure their arrival, many families had built shed-like structures in the back yard as living quarters for those who worked in the house. It was a hard life for them. When more and more American GI's arrived on the Base and were given passes to visit the various towns and resorts the domestics were happy because the Americans tipped generously.

At five o'clock I boarded the small tram, which was provided by the Jamaican Railroad. It held about 40 passengers and traveled on the same single track as the freight so it ran only after five p.m. on Friday and a scattered schedule on Saturday and Sunday. The last tram back to the Base on Sunday was at six p.m. After that there was no public transportation into the City and you had to travel by jeep or truck, as there were few motorcars on the island. The tram slowed often, at times coming to a stop, for the goats still had the right of way. Eventually we arrived at the Kingston station. Much to the dismay of the businessmen, the available taxi cabs would congregate at the station knowing that the train would arrive carrying American soldiers, and they would be able to double and triple their fares. Six of us jammed into the cab. We held on for dear life for not only did the Jamaicans drive on the wrong side of the road, the driver was master of the wheel. There was no boss to tell him what to do and he reminded me of the cabbies in New York City. We reached the USO without incident. A cement wall surrounded the grounds with barbed wire on the top. It was an accepted part of many buildings and homes as most of the crime was stealing. The gatekeeper waved the taxi through and we drove up to a covered portico of the one story wooden building with one main entrance. I was astounded. The foyer was tastefully decorated with rattan couches and chairs, the floor covered with a colorful rug, with side tables and lamps. Beyond could be seen a large dining area with round marble top tables on iron legs surrounded by four similar chairs as seen in soda parlors. Along the back wall was a counter divided into a soda fountain and a sandwich bar. Behind the counter there were more than a dozen native Jamaican young men in white coats, aprons, and white caps that were working the soda fountain, the grill and the stove. There were stools along the front of the counter and they were filled with servicemen, as were most of the tables. Again, I was surprised for I had assumed that the canteen would be open to only American servicemen but I soon found out that it was open to all servicemen including those serving in the British, Canadian, Australian and Jamaican Armed Forces. Leading off to the left of the lobby was a large dance floor with a bandstand and at the other side there were billiard tables. There was a reading room with well-stocked bookshelves lining the wall, which held the latest editions, a magazine rack and newspapers. This was a home away from home, I thought. Leave it to the Americans. No liquor or beer was served, only soft drinks. I knew that the Australians were paid on the same scale as we were, with the Canadians coming next. Then the English and then on the lower part of the scale came the Jamaicans. You could easily see why the USO was crowded with servicemen from the other countries. Everything could be had here, hot dogs, hamburgers, sandwiches of every description, French fries, ice cream sodas, sundaes and malt shakes. You name it; they had it. The supplies were flown in from the States and as we were not yet at war there was no rationing.

A short plump woman, with curly bright red hair, streaked with gray, greeted us. She wore a beautiful silk print dress and a string of pearls. Her name pin identified her as Miss Alice Mulally, USO Director. She welcomed us and told us to go to the registry desk and we would be given our bunk assignments. Then we were to take our duffel bags and we would be assigned a locker in the dormitories. We walked across the lawn to another long one story barracks. Like the main building there was but one entrance which I presumed was for security purposes. Near the door there was a curved reception desk on which stood a telephone system. An elderly white haired Jamaican wearing a white coat was seated behind the desk. His name pin identified him as Mr. Thomas McGregor, Dormitory Manager, USO. The name shook me for a moment but then I remembered in reading the history of Jamaica that among the many Englishmen who first arrived was a large contingent of Scots and Irish. Many of the slaves took the names of their masters and it was handed down from generation to generation. He had us sign our names in the register and gave us a small tab indicating the number of the bunk that we were to occupy. The long room was open and not divided. There were twenty steel cots, lining each side of the wall, covered with a mattress, sheets, blanket and a pillow. Next to each cot was a tall steel cabinet. It had one shelf for toilet articles and hooks for clothing. On the other side of the bed was a small end table. At the far end of the building were the toilets, showers and sinks. I stowed away my gear and hastened back to the main canteen.

Miss Mulally, who met me at the door, shook my hand and said, "Well, Sergeant Crouch, did you find everything OK?"

I was startled. "How did you know my name?"

"Come into my office."

She took me by the arm and led me into a spacious office. There were pictures on the walls and curtains on the window. She had a large wooden table that served as a desk. There was a telephone, intercom and papers scattered everywhere, and a smaller desk for her secretary. Several armchairs were in front of the desk. She told me to be seated as she went behind her desk and sat in a large leather back swivel chair.

"Colonel Ewing told me all about you, Sergeant," she said. Her eyes were bright and friendly. "The Colonel told me that you were organizing a group of servicemen to hold a Christmas party for the patients at the Spanish Town Leper Colony."

"Yes, that's true," I replied.

"If there is anything that I can do, Sergeant, I will be happy to do so. I also understand that you have visited there already." I nodded my head. "What was it like?" she said. "I don't think that I could take it."

"When you get over the initial shock it is easy," I said. "Once you look behind the mask of grotesque features you see a human being."

"That's a very good way of saying it, Sergeant. When are you scheduled to go there?"

"On Boxing Day. Sister said that is their traditional British day of exchanging gifts."

"What are you planning on doing?" she asked.

"It's all pretty well planned out. We are going to bring the Base Band to put on a show for them followed by refreshments—ice cream, cookies, candy, and soda. Then we will distribute the gifts. My Mom has already sent gifts for the 200 patients. She packed them in crates and the Army flew them down to the Base. They are now stored in the hospital."

"That's an ambitious undertaking. Your Mom purchased all of those gifts?"

"My Mom has a way about her. All she had to do was to suggest to her relatives and friends and they plunged right into the project." I tugged at my tie.

She looked at me and said, "You can loosen your tie, Sergeant. Your Mom sounds like mine, always willing to help." I loosened my tie. "Have you read the USO regulations McGregor gave you?"

I felt embarrassed and I remembered that he did give us a paper and I had just stuck it in my pocket.

"No, I'm afraid that I was so anxious to get back over here for a hot dog that I just put it in my pocket."

"Well, we do have regulations and we have to be pretty strict about them and one of them is bed time. The dormitory closes at midnight and no one is allowed in after that time. So you must remember that when you are out on the town. Then too, McGregor will not let anyone in who is inebriated or would cause trouble. He is a good man and used to be in the Jamaican Constabulary so he and his aides know how to handle people." She smiled.

"He is well built and although he has white hair I wouldn't want to tangle with him," I said. "But what happens to those who come back after twelve? Where do they stay?"

"There are many small hotels around here that will take them in. Sometimes the good people will offer them a bed." She looked down and there was a small tinge of red that crept into her face. "And there are plenty of not so good people who will offer them a bed. Often they wake up to find that their wallets are gone."

I knew what she was talking about as I had seen many servicemen come back from leave with bruises and black eyes and broke.

"I only had to pay $2.00 for the bed. How do you maintain such a beautiful place?" I now brought her back to familiar territory.

"The USO receives funds from both donations and the Government, and with the threats of war and more servicemen, donations have increased. Most of our staff are volunteers and we only charge a minimum amount for food and lodging. Everything else in the canteen is free."

"I noticed that many of the women have a ribbon marked Hostess on their lapel. Some seem to be very young while others. . . . " I didn't finish the sentence. She picked up a pen at her desk.

"Our hostesses are screened very carefully," she said. "We have more volunteers than we can handle. The young girls, many of them secretaries or teachers, find the USO a convenient place to meet nice young men."

"And not so nice," I muttered as I remembered some of the men who came into the dispensary, high on Gangi, the Jamaican marijuana, or with the D.T.'s from too much rum, and venereal disease from sneaking into the shantytown across from the Base. If they were caught they were punished either with confinement or hard labor. The flesh is weak.

She brought me back to reality when I heard, "What did you say, Sergeant?"

"Nothing, Miss Mulally."

"The older women are wives of businessmen and professionals who are bored since they can no longer travel to Europe or the States for vacations. Time lies heavy on their hands with so many servants to take care of their needs. This is their chance to do something for the war effort." She put down the pen. "If they take a shine to you, you will have a chance to see how the upper class lives." She paused, "I know that you are anxious to get that hot dog so I won't detain you any more but before you leave, tell me what you need for the patients at Spanish Town. By the way," she said, "the Colonel also told me that you have an R.N. degree and you are in charge of the operating room at the Base. We might call on you here."

"I hope not," I replied. "I want to get away from all of that for awhile if I can."

"I was kidding. We are very close to a good hospital in case we need medical help. Now go on and enjoy yourself."

She stood up. I shook her hand and went immediately to the soda fountain. My favorite luxury when I was growing up was to take the pennies I earned and go to the local soda fountain for a dish of vanilla ice cream covered with wet walnuts and chocolate syrup. I was hoping they served this here. I found an empty stool and described what I wanted.

The young man behind the counter said, "No trouble, Sergeant. We have all the fixings."

In no time he placed a dish before me with two scoops of vanilla ice cream covered with chocolate syrup and smothered with wet walnuts. I was in seventh heaven. After eating this, I lost my appetite for the hot dog. I went to the bulletin board to check the list of activities when I noticed the six piece orchestra unpacking their instruments and setting up on the stage in the dance hall. By now the place was crowded and I saw a listing that the Caribe was showing an English movie of Dickens' "Christmas Carol." I opted for that.

I walked to the theatre through crowded streets. Once again I was amused for the balcony seats were much more expensive than the orchestra. I figured that out. It was a means of segregation. The poor could afford the orchestra seats and those with more money the balcony seats. The theatre was spacious, beautifully decorated with tropical scenes, the seats plush and the air was cool. When the theatre darkened the first thing on the screen was a picture of the King, the British flag and the playing of their National Anthem, "God Save the King." As we all stood, I was waiting for the "Star Spangled Banner" but it never came. For the next two and half hours I was lost in the story of Ebenezer Scrooge and Tiny Tim as only the British actors could portray them.

I arrived back at the USO at eleven o'clock and went into the canteen. The dance band was finishing up their last set and I finally got my hot dog with sauerkraut. I wondered how that would set on my stomach during the night but who cares. I was on leave. By the time I had finished the crowd was beginning to file out. The band was packing away their instruments. The hostesses were waiting for their ride home. Some were strolling with GI's down the walk and through the gates. I'm sure that the night was just beginning for them. But I was tired and headed toward the dormitory. Half of the cots were filled when I entered. I was used to the lack of privacy. I took my toilet gear, went to the bathroom and brushed my teeth. Some of the GI's were fast asleep. Several others were gathered around playing cards on their bunk. I undressed, put my clothes in the steel cabinet and slipped under the covers. Nothing felt so luxurious to me. I put the pillow over my face to hide the bright lights from the ceiling and soon I was off asleep. I awoke once to find the room darkened. Heavy sighs mingled with snores. I got up to go to the bathroom, which was lit, and passed the desk where the night attendant was sitting. When I came back I noticed that there were two empty bunks. Some guys didn't make it. I wondered what would happen to them. I had learned from my months in the army to fall asleep at the drop of a hat, drowning out sounds all around me.

CHAPTER TWELVE

WHEN I AWOKE THE SUN WAS STREAMING in through the upper openings between the ceiling and the walls letting in the sounds and smells of a morning in Jamaica. It was Saturday and it was market day. I showered, shaved and dressed along with a few other GI's but most of them were still sleeping in their bunks. After dressing I went to the canteen. The cooks were already on duty. I did not see Mulally. When I asked where she was, the hostess on duty said that she was in her apartment. There was another building, which I had not noticed behind the main building that contained several apartments for members of the permanent USO staff. I looked at the menu posted behind the counter where the stoves were. It listed the same menu of hot dogs, hamburgers, all kinds of sandwiches and soup that I had seen the night before. I said to myself, I can't have a hot dog for breakfast. Then I smelled bacon and I saw the two cooks on duty making scrambled eggs, sausage, bacon and home fried potatoes. That was for me! Along with toast and two cups of coffee, I was set for the day. I looked at the list of activities available in the town. There were cricket matches, horse racing, church carnivals, several nightclubs with floor shows, movies, an open air band concert at Hope Gardens and art and flower shows. Almost like Saturdays at home. I then noticed church services at the Holy Cross Cathedral, the Anglican, the Episcopal, the Baptist, Seventh Day Adventist, the Presbyterian and other churches. The Synagogue held their services on Friday night. I had time to make the nine o'clock Mass. I was waiting in front for a cab when Miss Mulally drove up.

She rolled down the window and asked, "Where are you headed, Sergeant?"

"I'm trying to get to Mass at Holy Cross."

"I'm going there so hop in."

We arrived at the cathedral as Father entered the altar. There was only a handful at Mass. As we left the cathedral afterward, there was a priest dressed in a long black cassock shaking hands. Alice walked up to him and introduced me. His name was Father Thomas Feeney, S.J. and he was the Superior.

"Aha, Aha," he said. "So you are the Sergeant Crouch that I have been hearing about." He grasped my hand firmly. My name was really getting around.

He said, "Father Kiely has spoken about you."

So he is the one who is spreading the word. I will have to watch what I do or say, as it will get back to headquarters.

Father continued, "If you have a few moments why not come back to the rectory for a cup of coffee," and he turned to Alice and said, "You too, Alice."

She quickly replied, "Thank you, Father, but I have so many chores to do and I have a luncheon with the Jamaican League. They want to know more about what is going on in the USO."

I turned to her. "You go ahead, Mrs. Mulally, I mean Miss Mulally."

She laughed. "Remember, my name is Alice."

"My Mom wouldn't want me to call you by your first name. You go ahead. I will see you back at the USO sometime."

She shook Father Feeney's hand, patted me on the shoulder and was off. Father Feeney led me to the rectory behind the cathedral. It was quite a large building for a rectory but I found out that it contained many different sections. There was a large office as you entered the door and seated at the desk was a tall light skinned Jamaican woman with gray hair.

Father Feeney introduced her to me as Cissy Rowe and said, "She runs the place and keeps us in line."

Mrs. Rowe just smiled and said, "It is nice to meet you, Sergeant. Is this your first visit to Kingston?"

"Yes, Mrs. Rowe," I replied. "It is the first time that I have been able to visit since I landed in August."

Father then led me to the priests' quarters. On the way he told me that Mrs. Rowe was a very devout Catholic. She had two daughters and a son. Both daughters ran a dancing school, teaching ballet and other forms of dancing and were responsible for putting on the Christmas Pantomime as well as dance programs throughout the year. Her son was involved in real estate. During the rest of my stay in Jamaica I was often entertained at the Rowe home. They accepted me as a member of the family. The two girls were named Punky and Betty.

We entered the large refectory. There was a large crucifix on the wall and an oil painting of St. Ignatius of Loyola, the founder of the Jesuits. There was a long shiny mahogany table on which were placed straw placemats surrounded by twelve high back chairs. I noticed that the table could have seated many more. Father Feeney told me that members of the faculty of St. George as well as priests from the bishop's office resided here as well as the cathedral staff. He pointed to a chair, which was placed at the head of the table. I sat down. A dark Jamaican woman, neatly dressed in a black dress covered with a white apron, entered the room. She carried a pot of coffee that she placed on the mat near Father Feeney. She brought over cups and saucers, napkins and silverware, placing them before each of us. Father asked me if I would like to have eggs, bacon and toast.

I said, "No, Father, I had my breakfast at the USO."

"Well," he said. "You can't refuse Brother John's croissant. Not only is he our cook but he is also an excellent baker."

I perked up. "Croissants, I haven't had them in a long time. Those I will take."

The woman left and Father filled our cups with coffee.

He said, "Do you take milk and sugar?"

When I said, "Yes," he passed them to me.

He said, "I like my coffee black. It is Blue Mountain. There is no better coffee in the world. Now, tell me how things are going at the Army Base."

I began to tell him how everything is settling down and working smoothly and what a joy it was to have Father Kiely as our Chaplain. Then the door opened the woman entered again bearing two plates with two croissants on each and a small dish containing butter.

Father Feeney said, "Dig in, don't let them get cold."

For the next few minutes we ate silently as I relished the soft flaky croissants dripping with butter. They were the best that I ever tasted.

Father glanced at his watch. "Oh, my!" he said. "I must get going. I have a meeting with the Bishop. Perhaps I can drop you off somewhere."

"One of the women at the USO told me that I might be interested in just visiting the Saturday Market. Is that near by?" I said.

"It's on my way. It is a large shedded area with many stalls and there is a wide space for the vendors to spread their wares on a blanket on the ground. I would be careful of what you buy and eat for sanitation is not the best here. We thoroughly scrub all fruits and vegetables."

We left the rectory and went to the courtyard where there were three old Fords parked. It seemed that all of the priests drove Fords.

As we drove out of the courtyard he said, "You must be careful of the sun. It can cause much damage. Don't you have a pith helmet?"

"No, Father," I said. "I just have my cap. They did not issue pith helmets."

"Well, the least that you can do," he continued, "is to get yourself a pair of sunglasses. You will find them in the market. In fact you will find everything there from soup to nuts." He swerved to avoid hitting a pedestrian. "But I warn you be careful of what you pay. The listed price is just the starting point. They expect you to haggle. Once you enter the market, vendors shouting and screaming for you to buy their wares will surround you. Others are selling the same object and sometimes it ends up in fist fights over who is to get the sale."

He told me that he was not going up the street where the market was. It was too congested and he would lose time. He would leave me off about two blocks from the market and I could walk there. When he dropped me off he gave me a blessing and said that I would be seeing him again. When I neared the market, I saw that a large portion of it was under a slanted roof, open on all sides, with row after row of stalls. Another part was an open field where the women squatted over their wares displayed on tablecloths and blankets. It was truly a teeming mass of humanity. I wondered if I should even attempt to enter the area but I was in Jamaica and I wanted to experience as much as I could so that I would better understand the people. When they saw my uniform, women of all shapes, sizes, ages and forms of dress engulfed me. They pressed bunches of scallions, carrots and garlic toward me, screaming,

"Buy from me, soldier."

I was tempted to shove them aside, but I knew better as I am sure that it would have caused a riot. I was in their country now. I gently pushed my way towards the stalls and I saw every kind of vegetable imaginable. Jamaica did not lack for variety. There were eggplants, small tomatoes, string beans, onions, potatoes, squash, yams, grapefruit and akee (a certain portion of which I found was poisonous) and then there were fruits, pineapples, oranges, tangerines, pumpkins, melons of every kind, mangoes, papaya, and coconuts but no apples or pears. There was no semblance of order. In one stall would be East Indian sweets and in the next the pungent odor of fish. I did not gaze long at the meat stalls for there were slabs of red meat from goats, lamb from sheep, pork from pigs with pig ears, pig feet and even a pig head for sale. The meat was covered with swarming flies. Beef was not plentiful and there were few gathered around those stalls for the meat was very expensive. Chickens were sold live in crates. The smell, the sounds and the fury of the masses overwhelmed me and I had to leave after spending no more than half an hour. But that was enough. I would be careful of anything that I ate outside of the Base from now on. My uniform shirt was soaked with perspiration as I exited the market and headed for what looked like a soda stand. It was a small stand with a bright awning but it was doing a brisk business. There was lemonade, orangeade, soda pop, Red Stripe beer but I opted for a cold bottle of coke that was miraculously nestled in a bed of ice. No wonder the slogan, "The pause that refreshes," aptly describes the feeling when gulping down a coke.

I walked to the main shopping center. There were some tents under which sat Jamaican artists working on their easels. Many of the paintings were in watercolor. Other paintings were done in oil depicting scenes of Jamaican life. Some were crudely painted while others showed promise. There were scenes of the coast, the palm trees, plantations and Jamaican children and were all very interesting. I was told that Jamaican art was widely sought by tourists. Some of the shops had mahogany salad bowls and other items of mahogany, which was a widely used wood that would last a lifetime. By now, it was high noon and I had had enough. I finally hailed a taxi and went back to the quiet of the USO. I went first to the dormitory, greeted Tom, stripped off my clothes and headed for the shower. My bed was neatly made and I soon fell asleep. I awoke in a groggy state, for I must have slept deeply and it was quite warm even with the ceiling fans. After another shower I dressed in a clean uniform and walked over to the canteen, heading immediately to the counter and ordered a hamburger.

Then I remembered the meat in the market and told the cook, "Well done, please."

When the hamburger was sizzling, I told him to put a slice of cheese on it. He looked at me a little annoyed as if to say make up your mind, but he dutifully put on two slices of swiss cheese. The cheeseburger was placed on a platter, containing two slices of pickle, a heaping helping of French fries and a slice of tomato on a piece of lettuce. Remembering the market, I ignored the tomato and lettuce but then thought Mulally would not allow contaminated food to be served in the canteen. I took my plate to an empty table, went over to the soda fountain and ordered a large chocolate milkshake. As I ate the hamburger and gulped the milkshake, I thought of Father Kiely, and the times that I had griped about how difficult it was to be in the Army. I smiled as I thought of what he would have to say if he saw me now.

The USO was beginning to fill up. I did not see too many Americans, but there were groups of British, Canadian and Australian soldiers along with Officers. Some ate with their enlisted men but I noticed the English Officers were off to themselves. Some wore red berets and carried what looked like riding crops. They were not very friendly and I surmised that they were not happy with the Americans staying out of the war. Back in the States, there was still opposition to becoming involved with the war in Europe and there were still many who resented Roosevelt for signing the Lend-Lease Agreement, supplying ammunition and equipment to England, which they believed, would eventually draw us into the conflict. Groups of men were playing billiards. Others were reading in the library. In the dance hall a young girl, surrounded by a group of men, was seated at the piano, singing. I grabbed a copy of Time magazine, which had just arrived by plane from the States and I sank back in a cushioned armchair in the foyer to catch up on the news.

One of the older hostesses, a handsome woman, came over and sat down beside me. She introduced herself as Kathleen Swaby. She asked how I was doing and what were my impressions of Jamaica. I told her how fascinated I was with the people and their customs as well as the beauty of the island. She told me that her husband was one of the leading attorneys on the island. They lived up in the hills outside of Kingston. She wanted to know if I was doing anything that evening and if not, she would be delighted to have me as a guest for dinner in her home. I jumped at the idea and she told me that she would send her car to pick me up at seven thirty. Mulally was right. There was an opportunity to mingle with the upper classes. Soon Miss Mulally came in and invited me to have tea with her in her office. We sat opposite each other on the comfortable chairs and her secretary brought in a tray with a silver tea pot, two cups and saucers, a silver sugar bowl with tongs with small cubes of sugar and a small silver pitcher with milk. On the plate were scones and pastries. Alice looked tired and I asked her how the meeting went with the Jamaican women.

"Perfect," she said. "Luncheon was delicious and there was a great deal of interest in the USO. They asked me many questions and more and more volunteers signed up. I don't know how we can use all of them as some of them can only give a few hours a week." She took a sip of tea. "How did your day go? Did you get to the market?"

"It was a fantastic experience." I said. Munching on a cookie, I asked her, "Have you ever gone to one of those markets?"

"No," she said, "And from what I have heard, I don't intend to go."

"Well," I said, "I am glad that I had the experience because it gave me an insight as to how these poor people have to fight for even a few pennies."

"And how did your talk go with Father Feeney?" she asked.

I replied, "He didn't have very much time as he had an appointment to see the Bishop but he did take me to the market and dropped me off."

I took a sip of tea. I was not very fond of tea. The cookies were good. In the months to come, High Tea was an event to look forward to. It was a perfect way to relax at the end of a hard workday and it would be several hours before dinner.

"Father Feeney is a brilliant man and he has studied all of the superstitions of the people of the West Indies." She took another sip of tea.

"What are your plans for the evening?"

"I am excited. Remember you told me that there were several wealthy women of the upper class who were hostesses and yet if they took a shine to you they would invite you to their homes. Well, I have been invited to Kathleen Swaby's home for dinner."

"Wonderful," she said. "Kathleen is a charming woman and her husband, Leonard, is a graduate of Harvard Law School and Kathleen is from Ireland. Wait until you see their home as they have a spectacular view of Kingston."

"I will have to watch my table manners," I said and Alice chuckled.

"They are not like the upper crust English. They are down to earth and Leonard's years in the United States have Americanized him."

After tea, Alice went back to her apartment to get ready for the evening crowd. I went back to the dormitory to make sure that I was properly groomed

McGregor was on duty and when he saw me looking into the mirror, he smiled and said, "Hot date tonight, Sergeant?"

I flushed. "No, I am going to dinner with one of the hostesses." I emphasized, "And with her husband."

McGregor shook his head and mumbled something in the Jamaican lingo which I did not understand but what I guessed was similar to, tell me another! I waited by the steps of the canteen and right on the dot of seven, a shiny black Cadillac sedan drove up driven by a young Jamaican in a chauffeur's cap. He pulled up in front of the canteen, stopped and got out of the car. He came around to the side of the car and asked if I were Sergeant Crouch. He then opened the back door. By now there were GI's standing around and staring at me. I was embarrassed. I asked the driver if I could sit up front.

He looked perplexed but then he said, "Yes, Sir." He opened the front door and I slid in next to the driver.

As we left the gates of the USO compound I turned to him and said, "What is your name?"

"Simeon."

We headed through the crowded streets of Kingston. Simeon smiled as he saw me grasping the strap on the door, hanging on for dear life. I still could not get used to driving on the left side of the road. I glanced at Simeon and gave him a sheepish smile. He was a young man, light skin, very handsome. His trim build fitted the neatly pressed chauffeur's uniform with the jaunty cap. I tried to strike up a conversation but all that I got in reply was a "Yes, Sir," or a "No, Sir." I stopped trying for it was evident that he was well trained not to engage in conversation with his passengers. As we entered the outskirts of the City, there were more and more modest bungalows, spacious yards, all fenced in.

Then we began our ascent up the winding roads, hugging the sides of the Blue Mountains. The higher we went the cooler it became. The road was only wide enough for two cars going in opposite directions. There were hairpin turns, which were guarded by what looked like to me flimsy rails to keep one from falling off the precipice. On the left side of the road there were large banks of ferns, trees and flowering shrubs of every color and description. Here and there would be a wide break revealing a substantial house with lush lawn and tailored grounds. Three quarters of the way up the mountain we pulled in off the main road through a stone gate, guarded by a heavy chain. Simeon stopped the car, got out and unhooked the chain. We rode up a short distance of a gravel path when Simeon stopped again and went back to lock the gate. I still could not see the house. Fifty yards further we took another turn and there it stood atop a grassy knoll. It was a sprawling brick structure all on one level. A portico covered the driveway. Simeon stopped the car, got out and opened my door.

CHAPTER THIRTEEN

TWO LARGE MAHOGANY RED IRISH SETTERS came bounding down the steps. Simeon told me not to worry. They were friendly, but I was not sure. They came up to me wagging their tails and brushing against my legs. Surrounding the entire front and both sides of the house was a covered veranda. Behind the house I could see the top of the Blue Mountains, now covered in light mist. A series of stone steps led up to the veranda on which were clusters of white wicker armchairs, glass top cocktail tables and baskets of ferns. A low stone balustrade ran the length of the open sides of the veranda. Soon the glass doors opened and Kathleen came sweeping out. She wore a form-fitting red silk cocktail dress. Around her throat was a single strand of pear shaped diamonds. Her abundant bright red hair was swept back from her face and was tied with a red satin bow. In her ears she wore two large pear shaped diamonds. Her pale skin was dotted with attractive freckles and her bright blue eyes marked the finishing touches of a beautiful Irish woman. She waited at the top of the stairs to greet me. She led me to a cluster of chairs. The cushions were covered in a beautiful knitted cloth on which were embroidered huge red hibiscus flowers.

She said, "Leonard will be with us shortly."

I walked to the railing and gazed out at the breathtaking view. Far below me lay the city of Kingston. I could make out certain landmarks, the Palisadoes Airport, the harbor and the Myrtle Bank Hotel. Kathleen stood beside me.

"Breathtaking, isn't it?" she said. "I never get used to it and later on when the sun sets it will be even more spectacular."

Just then the door opened and Leonard came out onto the veranda. He was a medium built man deeply tanned. He was dressed in black tuxedo pants, white dress shirt, black bow tie and a beautiful tailored white silk jacket. His thick pure white hair was combed straight back. He put out his hand and grasped mine firmly but gently.

"So this must be the Sergeant that Kathleen has been telling me all about."

I was not used to being entertained in such elegance. First thing that I could remember to say was "You have a beautiful home."

"It's comfortable," he said, as a matter of fact.

After we were seated around the cocktail table, the door opened again and a young slim Jamaican, wearing a short white jacket, white bow tie and dark trousers came over to us. Kathleen introduced him as Malcolm.

Leonard said, "What would you like to drink, Sergeant?"

My Mother had taught me when invited out to dinner to let the host make the suggestion. This caused fewer embarrassments.

So I said, "Whatever you are having, Sir."

He laughed. "This is not the Army, call me Leonard."

"OK," I said. "Then you can call me Howard."

"We have whatever you like." He said, "I am having a scotch old fashioned."

"Great," I said quickly. "I would enjoy one of those. We only have beer and rum at the canteen."

"And you, Kathleen?" he said turning to her.

She looked at Malcolm and said, "Make it three on the rocks."

Malcolm gave a short bow, turned smartly and left the veranda. Leonard removed a slim silver cigarette case from inside his jacket pocket, opened it and offered me a cigarette. I wanted to act sophisticated but I knew from past experience that cigarettes and I did not agree and I would embarrass myself by choking.

I said, "I'm sorry but I don't smoke."

"Don't be sorry. Be grateful that you haven't taken up this bad habit. Kathleen and I have no willpower. Does our smoking bother you?"

"Oh no, sir. I have gotten used to it. Everybody in my barracks smokes."

He took out a cigarette lighter, held it to Kathleen's cigarette and then his own. Malcolm came out bearing a tray with three crystal tumblers. He placed a glass in each of the trays on our chairs and presented us each with a white linen napkin.

Leonard lifted his drink and said, "Cheers."

We clicked our glasses together. It was one of the best drinks that I had ever tasted.

Kathleen said, "I was going to invite some of our friends to join us but Leonard was so anxious to hear what was going on in the States, we decided not to share you with anyone."

Leonard started off by asking me what the latest news was. I told him that I had been in Jamaica since August so I had lost contact. At the Base we only received a one page daily bulletin.

Leonard then asked, "When did you enlist?"

"Oh, I didn't enlist. I was drafted."

"Oh, I didn't think that they sent draftees out of the States."

I then explained to him how I was pulled out of basic training to join the medical group headed for Jamaica.

Leonard then said, "Do you believe that America will get into the war?"

"I don't think so. There is so much anti-war sentiment in the United States but with Churchill and Roosevelt agreeing to that Lend-Lease Plan, the increased call-up of draftees and new Army Bases springing up around the country, most people think that war will be inevitable."

By now it had grown dark and the lights of Kingston below were more clearly visible. Even ships in the harbor were strung with lights.

"I read so much about blackouts in London and the nightly air raids. Aren't you afraid here in Jamaica with all of these lights lit that you might be a target for the Luftwaffe?"

Leonard replied. "Except for shipping lanes and our proximity to the Panama Canal, I don't believe that Jamaica is a threat to Germany." He knocked out his cigarette in the ashtray. "Our only fear is a Commando raid from a submarine. But we have little in the way of war materials that they could destroy. We have no munitions factory or vital supplies except for the sugar." He thought a moment. "However, with the building of the Air Base out at Fort Simonds and more and more Navy reconnaissance planes equipped with ammunition and Army bombers arriving, the threat might be heightened. I also hear from friends of mine who work with the British garrison here that Britain is uneasy about the squabbles the United States is having with Japan."

Kathleen said, "I'm not aware of any of that."

I said, putting down my empty glass, "I'm sure that if there were any threats our Commander would have let us know."

I wanted to lift out the maraschino cherry and a slice of orange from my glass but thought it would be impolite until I saw Kathleen remove hers. Malcolm then came out to announce that dinner was served. It was getting chilly since cool air was drifting down from the top of the mountains. If I thought that the veranda was luxurious, the house itself was breathtaking. The living room was spacious with mahogany floors, beautiful Victorian furniture covered in rich brocades. To the rear was a long dining room with windows overlooking another covered veranda. A garden led to the base of the hill. Beyond were the beautiful Blue Mountains. I could see flowering trees, bushes, beds of roses, blue delphiniums and almost every other flower imaginable. This accounted for the many vases of flowers scattered about the living room and on the dining room table, which could seat fifteen. In the center of the table were two candelabras on either side of a large bowl of tea roses. We passed through the dining room to the back veranda, which was enclosed with glass windows.

A small round dining room table, covered in a white linen tablecloth, was set for three. Overhead was a beautiful Tiffany lamp. There were three comfortable armchairs and in front of each was a beautiful place setting of Spode china in the Indian Tree pattern. Highly polished silverware at each side of the plates, and in front of each setting were crystal goblets. We overlooked the gardens and the Blue Mountains, over which rose a full pale yellow moon, which made one think that we were in Shangri-la. After we were seated at the table, Malcolm poured a sparkling pale yellow Chardonnay into the wine glass.

Leonard lifted his glass and said, "Long life!" Once again we clinked glasses.

I was not a connoisseur of wines and I asked, "Is this from France?"

"No," Leonard said. "It's a California Chardonnay."

I thought that this was strange until I realized that there was no embargo from the United States. They just could not get goods from Europe. Leonard had made many friends while at Harvard and they kept him well supplied with American goods sent by air cargo from Florida.

Both Malcolm and the second man, whose name was Robert, left the room. Robert returned with a large silver tray and a crystal dish, heaped high with a variety of sliced fruit and a silver ladle server. He first came to my side and held out the tray for me to scoop out some fruit into the top dish of the stack of dishes before me. I thought that it was strange that he did not go to Kathleen first. The guest was the first to be served. I knew that I was awkward and spilled some of the fruit from the top dish to the second. I saw that neither Leonard nor Kathleen was looking at me. It would be the height of ill manners to embarrass a guest. The fruit had been chilled and was delicious. Malcolm came in and cleared the plates. Robert reappeared with another silver tray on which stood a porcelain soup tureen. I was shaken, as I knew that I would spill the soup but fortunately Robert ladled the soup into my soup plate. I waited until Kathleen and Leonard had their soup to see which utensil they would pick up. It was easy to spot the soupspoon as it was much like the ones that we had at home. I noticed that they filled their spoon by drawing the soup away from them instead of drawing it toward them and I followed suit.

I had never tasted this type of soup before but when Kathleen said, "Have you had pumpkin soup before?" it saved me from embarrassment.

"No," I said. "It is delicious."

"It is a common dish in the Caribbean and each island has their own variety. I like the pumpkin soup better than some that contain fish or other ingredients," Kathleen said.

"I would be interested in knowing the recipe," I said. "I could get our chef at the Army Base to make it."

"It is simple," Kathleen said. "The main ingredient is pureed fresh pumpkin. There is chicken stock and the key is to know the right amount of spices. I will be glad to give you the recipe."

The courses were served in succession accompanied by interesting conversation. Leonard told me about the cases that he was involved with. Kathleen was interested in the theatre and missed her trips to London and New York. I, for the most part, listened. My Mom had always taught us that if you want to learn anything you must listen. Leonard was interested in what was going on at the Army Base. The third course was a filet of red snapper fish, sautéed in butter and sprinkled with chives. It was served on what to me looked like a salad plate. Again I watched and I saw that Kathleen picked up what looked like a butter knife. I did the same and found out later that what we use as a butter knife, they use as a fish knife. Malcolm then filled the wine glasses with burgundy and removed the red snapper which was tasty, flaky and without bones. Robert brought in a huge platter on which stood a crown roast of beef. Leonard stood up and Robert handed him a carving knife and a long fork. Robert removed our large plate on which Leonard had placed a large thick slice of beef which was well done at the edges and pink in the center. Malcolm brought in a tray with several Spode dishes filled with various vegetables. The more that I looked at the Spode, the more I thought of how Mom would love something like this and Kathleen informed me that the Spode was available in the stores of the islands. Both Leonard and Kathleen ate their meal in the manner of the English keeping the fork in their left hand and the knife in their right, using their knife to push the various foods onto the fork. It was too awkward for me so I kept changing the knife and the fork.

Leonard smiled and said, "When I was at Harvard I had an awkward time. So I know what you are going through. Just relax and be yourself. I still have trouble mashing the peas on the fork."

Kathleen giggled. I knew that she was trying to make me feel comfortable.

She said, "I remember hearing somewhere that you could always tell an American by the way he held his knife and fork and if he asked for ice cubes in his water."

At the end of the meal we returned into the living room and on the way Leonard asked if I wished to wash my hands and I said no that I was fine. I lost the opportunity to explore the rest of the house. When we were seated in the living room, Leonard opened a wooden box and the smell of cigars permeated the room. Leonard handed the box to me.

He said, "This is the finest quality that Jamaica makes. You should try one."

So I took one out and he took his and using a small instrument, he snipped off the end of the cigar and then handed the instrument to me. I followed suit. Then using a lighter he lit the end and puffed vigorously until it glowed and handed the lighter to me. I tried to follow suit but began to choke.

Kathleen said, "That's enough, Sergeant. Don't try to be polite and choke to death."

I was grateful and said, "I will just hold it in my hand, if you don't mind. I love the smell."

Kathleen lifted out a cigarette from a silver cigarette case lying on a table near her. She put it in a long cigarette holder and lit it. I felt out of place. Malcolm then entered with a decanter of brandy and a decanter of port wine.

He asked, "Would you like brandy or port wine, Sir?"

I said, "I will take the brandy."

He handed me a large brandy glass and deftly poured enough to fill the bottom. Kathleen took port while Leonard took brandy. I warmed the brandy in my hands and I sniffed it as I had seen it done in the movies. Leonard finally brought the topic around to what I had been thinking through the course of the evening.

"I'm sure you are thinking, Sergeant," taking a sip of his brandy and a puff of his cigar, "that we eat like this everyday and you're wondering about rationing."

I did not want to admit that I was thinking the same thing but was too polite to say anything.

"Our deprivations come in other ways," he said. "Travel restrictions are very tight. There is a law against sending money to our relatives and friends abroad. English imports are becoming scarce and I could go on and on. We each must make our sacrifices in our own way."

"That's true," I said. "I'm in the Army where we must do without necessities and luxuries, yet here I am living on a Base in Jamaica surrounded by beautiful palms. We have very comfortable living quarters, a movie theatre, a swimming pool and even Jamaican help in our kitchen, tending our yards and many officers have maids. Our food is excellent. We also have recreational clubs and bars. Yet everyone is griping because of the isolation." I took a sip of brandy. "But of course we are not at war."

"Not yet, anyway," Leonard said.

I did not like the sound of those words. Kathleen looked at me.

"Do you have apples at the Base?" she asked.

"Yes, I have seen some," I said. "Would you like me to bring some when I come in the next time?"

"I would love an apple," Kathleen said. "It is the one thing that I miss."

A foggy mist was coming off the mountains and Kathleen said, "It's almost eleven o'clock and I know that you have to be back to the dorm by twelve. If you wait too much longer we will be fogged in."

"Simeon is a good driver. You don't have to worry," said Leonard. "He will stay with his family in Half Way Tree and bring the car back in the morning."

"That makes me feel better because I was feeling guilty about making him drive under dangerous conditions."

Leonard laughed. "Every hour of the day presents dangerous conditions for a driver but one thing that you will get to know is that these Jamaicans have great reflexes."

I rose and Leonard and Kathleen escorted me to the door.

As they stood on the veranda, I said, “I don’t know how to thank you for one of the most wonderful evenings that I can ever remember.”

Kathleen walked me to the car.

On the way she said, “Sergeant, thanks for such an interesting evening. Leonard doesn’t speak very much at our dinner meetings. He has so much on his mind and must keep so much of what he does secret that many people think of him as a snob.” She laughed. “He is far from that. He is a fun loving guy if he is with the right people.”

“I found him very interesting and easy to get along with and I thank you again. I won’t forget to bring the apples the next time I come into Kingston. It is wonderful what you are doing at the USO,” I said, as I once again shook her hand.

She drew closer to me and kissed me on the cheek. “Working at the canteen really gives me a feeling that I am contributing something in this terrible war. You must come again.”

This time Simeon opened the passenger side door for me and I slipped inside. As we backed down the driveway, I leaned out and waved. Kathleen stood there waiting while we went through the gate onto the main road. I did not realize it then but it would be many months before I could bring those apples into Kingston. The headlights glowed through the fog and all the way down the hillside we did not encounter a single car. Even the goats were asleep. The streets of Half Way Tree were mostly deserted except for clusters of people in front of the bars. I was thoroughly satiated and mentally stimulated when Simeon dropped me off at the USO dormitory. I shook his hand, thanked him for being such an excellent driver and slipped a five-pound note into his pocket. I knew that this was more than what he made for a week or even two weeks but I was happy to show my appreciation in this way.

One of McGregor’s staff was on duty and asked, “Did you have a good time, Sergeant?”

I did not think he knew where I had spent the evening, probably like the majority of other GI's on leave, exploring the bars and other places seeking pleasure. I quickly undressed, brushed my teeth and slipped under the covers of my bunk. At the same time hundreds of miles from Jamaica on the Island of Oahu in the Hawaiian chain, thousands of sailors were crowding the streets, the shops, the restaurants and the bars along Waikiki Beach, leaving their ships lightly manned. They were enjoying the hospitality of the Hawaiians, a most gracious and fun loving people. I was the only one turning in at eleven p.m. on a Saturday night and slept so soundly that I did not hear anyone enter until I heard the crowing of a rooster.

CHAPTER FOURTEEN

I AWOKE TO FIND THE EARLY MORNING LIGHT filtering through the windows. I looked around me and every cot was filled. It was only five o'clock so I lay there quietly so as not to wake the sleepy men and soon was back in dreamland. I awoke with a start and I heard men stirring around shuffling back and forth into the bathroom. I looked at my watch. It was nine a.m. I had overslept for I had planned to attend the eight a.m. Mass. It was Sunday, December 7, 1941, four months since I had landed in Jamaica. I hastily left my bunk before my morning ablutions, dressed and headed for the canteen. It was more quiet than usual. The markets and shops were closed and most people on the street were dressed in their Sunday clothes hastening to various church services. I had a good breakfast with pleasant thoughts of the night before. The leave had been a welcome relief from the monotony of the Base and I would have to catch the five p.m. tram back to the Base so I planned to spend the afternoon at a cricket match after attending the noon Mass at the Cathedral. After breakfast, I strolled the grounds of the USO Compound. I met up with a few GI's who told me of their escapades on Saturday night, not worth repeating. To be one of the guys I made up a story of my barhopping. If they only knew of the enchanting evening that I had spent with the Swabys. They would think that I was off my rocker spending time in uplifting conversation instead of pursuing the pleasures offered by the City of Kingston. I started to walk toward the Cathedral when a car pulled up and one of the hostesses with her husband and family offered me a lift. They too were going to the noon Mass.

The Cathedral was almost filled and even the poorest Jamaican was dressed in Sunday finery. All of the women wore hats and the men suits. It was a High Mass. There was a large choir in the loft. The altar was aglow with candles and baskets of flowers. The celebrant was to be Bishop Emmett. There was a procession down the middle aisle of altar boys and acolytes in red cassocks, followed by four priests. Then came the Bishop, in his beautiful vestments, with miter on his head and carrying the staff representing the Shepherd of his flock. The choir sang beautifully. The Jamaicans might lack many of the necessities of life but one thing they loved was singing, music and dancing. After the homily and the Consecration, a priest strode to the altar, spoke to the Bishop and then proceeded to the pulpit and microphone.

He said, “With the Bishop’s permission I interrupt this Mass to make an announcement. All members of the United States Forces are to return to Fort Simonds immediately. Trucks will be available at the USO Compound.”

I turned to my friends and looked startled and said, “Something serious must have happened.”

I left the pew and as I reached the vestibule there were three M.P.’s standing at the door. Their jeeps were waiting at the entrance. There was a handful of G.I.’s at the Mass and we were ushered into the jeeps.

I turned to the M.P., who was driving and said, “What’s up? What’s happened?”

“Well,” he said, “You will find out.”

He deposited us back at the USO Compound and other jeeps arrived with soldiers and then there was a convoy of Army trucks. Other than the G.I.’s and the hostesses, the USO and the staff were the only ones around. Military personnel from the Jamaican, Australian and Canadian barracks were also ordered to return to their headquarters. There was an eerie silence and I saw a few of the hostesses in tears. I quickly went to Alice who was sobbing. Her face was ashen and she was shaking.

I blurted out, "What's happened? Why doesn't somebody tell us what has happened?"

She blurted out, "Pearl Harbor has been bombed."

"Pearl Harbor," I said. "Is that near our Base?"

"No, no, Pearl Harbor is in Hawaii where the Fleet is stationed and the Japanese sneak attack has sunk or damaged severely nearly every ship in the harbor. Thousands of service men have been killed. Oh, my God, what will happen to us?"

I took her in my arms and tried to console her. I was too stunned to really comprehend what had happened. Soon an officer from Fort Simonds drove up in a jeep and everyone was ordered to stand at attention.

In a loud shaky voice he said, "Pearl Harbor has been attacked. We must return to the Base immediately. Board the trucks."

I kissed Alice on the cheek and said, "Don't worry. We will handle it."

I left to board the truck. We were silent on the way back to the Base, each buried in his own thoughts. The driver told us that he had heard that not only was the Fleet destroyed but also all of the planes at Hickam Field had been put out of commission.

He said, "There is pandemonium in the States."

We are at war, I thought. This is it. Just last night Leonard had said that it would not be long before America would be at war. What will happen? Will I be shipped back home? I wonder what the family is doing and on and on my thoughts rambled until we pulled up at the gates of the Base.

Soldiers were everywhere and dressed in battle garb with steel helmets, guns fixed with bayonets. It was almost like a scene out of a war movie. As we disembarked we were told to quickly get to our units. I ran to the hospital. I found the entire staff assembled in the small auditorium. Captain Holland was addressing the group. I entered through the back door and slid into a seat. We had rehearsed every week the plan he had devised in case of a catastrophe. Each member of the unit knew exactly what to do. He passed out assignments. Members of the staff would work in shifts around the clock. Medics were not permitted to carry arms. He gave some instructions on blackout procedures, which would begin at dusk. All lights were to be extinguished, except for the operating and emergency room that had been equipped with dark shades. Not even a match was to be lit outdoors. No one knew what would happen next. Would the Japanese bomb the Fort? The patrol for the airfield would be doubled and no one was to leave their quarters except to fulfill their duties and the Base would be closed so that no one would enter or leave during the blackout. After the meeting we were dismissed to attend to our duties.

I went to the operating room with one of the Army nurses and we checked all of the emergency supplies. The hospital chef had prepared a cold supper that we ate from paper plates. I did not know if a blackout would be effective for there was a full moon and I knew that there would be fires and lamps lit in the shantytown across from the Base. We had only four in-patients. There were plenty of beds available in case of an emergency but most of our thoughts were of home. I could only imagine what each household was going through. Later in a letter from Mom she told me that the whole family had gathered together and that there was a great deal of tension, many prayers, especially for me.

CHAPTER FIFTEEN

THE NEXT DAY ROOSEVELT DECLARED WAR on Japan and later on, Germany and Italy. Rumors spread through shantytown that the airfield would be bombed and there was a large exodus. I wondered whether Grace and her Granny were still there. Back in the States, the nation was plunged into war activity. Recruitment stations were filled with young and old men trying to enlist. My brother Bob went into the Navy and my younger brother, Lou, was still in high school. It was America's finest hour. The women left their jobs as teachers, stenographers and homemakers to work in the factories building up our war supplies. I worried about the Christmas party for the leprosy patients. I was sure that it would be cancelled. I would get the gifts somehow to Spanish Town. In the next few weeks more Navy patrol planes arrived. A contingent of Coast Guard arrived to be stationed at hastily built barracks on a small island, known as Goat Island, to guard the harbor. A small first aid station and dispensary with several hospital beds was set up on the island and I was sent there to get things in readiness. The Coast Guard was joined by a contingent of Marines and artillery. More troops arrived for Fort Simonds. Captain Holland was shipped back to the states to establish a training center for medical corpsmen at Camp Barkley, Texas. A Major Douds, who was an ear, nose and throat specialist along with two more doctors, Captain Effler and Lieutenant Wein, replaced him. They were both surgeons and Lieutenant. Wein had just completed his internship.

After a few weeks the blackouts were cancelled. Christmas was spent relatively quiet and subdued. Everyone's thoughts were back in the United States. Father Kiely celebrated Mass. I asked him if he had seen either Grace or her Granny and he said no but he would let me know if they came to church and he would give them their gifts.

The Colonel saw no reason why we should cancel our Christmas party at the Leprosarium since he knew the patients were eagerly awaiting the day. So everything went ahead as scheduled. Three truckloads of soldiers and supplies took off in the morning of Boxing Day. We had notified the Sisters that we were coming and they had put up some Christmas decorations. The patients were all dressed in their best and the auditorium was filled. The band set up their instruments and when they started to play the auditorium emptied! Puzzled at first, we saw that everyone was out on the lawn dancing and swaying to the music. That made the musicians only play harder. Soon they all filed back in and the gifts were handed out. Mom had done a good job. Everything was gaily wrapped. Some patients did not tear off the paper and the ribbons as my nieces and nephews did when they gather around the tree at home. They carefully removed the wrappings, smoothed them out and put them in a pocket and rolled up the ribbons. There were "Oh's" and "Ah's" but not many compared their gifts with one another. They immediately put them in the bags they carried. Possessions were not shared and they hoarded their gifts. Then came the refreshments. Many had never eaten ice cream and at the first spoonful almost spit it out, as it was so cold. When I next visited, the poor Sisters told me that they had a difficult time in calming everyone down after we left.

As we drove out of the gate, many of the patients shouted, "God bless dem Americans."

Driving back home one of the soldiers started to sing, "Silent Night." We all joined in. It must have caught on for we heard echoes of our songs coming from the other trucks. When we entered the gates of the Fort we were tired, sweaty, dusty and our throats were hoarse but we had been given a spirit that held all the meaning of Christmas. When word spread around of the good time that we all had had, those who did not go asked how they could get to the Leprosarium and from then on it became a stopping off point on their way on a pass into Kingston. We were restricted to the Base for the next three months. Father told me that Grace and her Granny had not shown up for Christmas and when I looked across the road I would search for Grace but she was not there. I told Father to give their gifts to some poor people in the parish.

In order to keep us alert there were many drills, even staged mock landings on the beaches. The Fort was still heavily patrolled. The only signs of war were the constant noise of the patrol planes taking off and landing. With America now at war, the U-boats slackened off and there were few sightings from our reconnaissance planes. One directive amused us all. In order to give us some experience as to what our buddies were facing overseas in the war zone, all of the mess halls and canteens were closed on Mondays and we were issued a pack of K-rations consisting of dried beef, turkey, dried biscuits, dried soup to be mixed with water, and the like. We wisened up and on Sunday we stored extra food in our footlocker and gave the K-rations to the poor Jamaicans who seemed to enjoy them.

Monotony set in and Colonel Ewing was aware of the restlessness of the troops and the leave restrictions were lifted. He then planned various trips to beautiful spots in Jamaica, which was the playground of the rich and famous before the war. These included Ocho Rios on the north shore and especially to the Shore Park Hotel, perched on a hill overlooking the ocean with easy access to Dunn's River Falls. It was set by a large waterfall, which rushed over rocks and emptied into the sea. One could swim in the warm salty Caribbean and walk over to the falls and have a delightful ice cold shower. Then there was Montego Bay, the jewel of Jamaica. There were several lavish hotels, including the Casablanca, which had catered to the rich and now were happy to have the G.I.'s, even though we paid only one-tenth of what they formerly charged. USO troops began to visit us occasionally and we formed our own theatre club that I was placed in charge of and we produced plays and skits, using the varied talent available on the Base.

Then one Sunday in May, I had planned to go bike riding with five of my buddies to a fishing village on the coast some ten miles from the Base. It was my favorite form of recreation. The road was not paved but consisted of hard packed red clay. This soil was prevalent in many parts of Jamaica and was excellent for growing things. The road was lined with palm trees, giant banyan, mahogany and tall bamboo. Halfway to the sea was the Milk River Baths in a large concrete building. Inside it was divided into many pools of different sizes, fed by large streams of water containing sulfur from many springs. It was considered to be a Health Spa as the water had healing powers. It was widely frequented by businessmen and the elderly. On the way back from our visit to the fishing village and a dip in the sea, we would stop at the baths to bathe in the clear waters of the pools despite the heavy smell of sulfur. There was a restaurant and a bar attached where I would get a chicken sandwich and an ice cold Coca-Cola to quench my thirst after the long and dusty bike ride.

CHAPTER SIXTEEN

ON THIS SUNDAY MORNING IN MAY, as we left the gates of the Fort I could not believe my eyes, for there, squatting over a basket of fruit, was Grace. I told my companions to go along and I would catch up with them, that I was having trouble with the bike. After they had passed out of sight I walked my bike over to where Grace was squatting. In front of her was a straw basket filled with mangoes. She wore a faded gray dress with several patches of a pink material. Her feet were bare and on her head she wore a red bandana from which strands of straight black hair had escaped. Her face was scrubbed clean and she could easily pass for a little white girl. Her nose was small and pert, her lips thin, her wide luminous eyes a soft brown. As I approached her she drew back a little. I could see that she was frightened. She sat apart from the other vendors. I imagine that she was not fully accepted by them because of her skin color.

I walked up to her and said, "Grace?"

She looked startled, and said nothing. I repeated, "Your name is Grace, isn't it?"

Almost in a whisper, she said, "Yes."

To reassure her, I told her that Father Kiely had told me her name. She smiled. I said, "You know Father Kiely, don't you?" She nodded her head vigorously.

I did not want to frighten her any more so I handed her several shillings and said, "I don't need any mangoes but here you take this and buy some sweets."

She stood up and said, “No, no, my Granny would not like me to do that.”

“Your Granny,” I said. “Where is she?”

She pointed back to the shantytown. “She told me that I must not take any money unless you take the mangoes.”

I said, “OK, give me two.”

She produced a paper bag in which she placed the two mangoes.

I said, “You tell your Granny that the Sergeant would like to see her. Can you remember that?”

Again she nodded her head and put the shillings in her pocket. I reached out to pat her head but then pulled back. I would take it easy and not rush things. I felt triumphant, as I had at last made contact with this beautiful waif.

I caught up with my companions who had stopped to fix a flat on one of their bikes. We then proceeded to the sea. After a brief swim and our usual stop back at the Milk Baths we returned to the Base exhausted but rejuvenated. I glanced at the spot where Grace had been selling her wares and she was gone. Several days later Sergeant McGuire had to drive into May Pen to pick up some supplies and took me along as a passenger. It would give me an opportunity to stop off and see Father Kiely. As we left the gates of the Base, I noticed Grace squatting in her usual spot. I told McGuire to stop. Although we were not permitted to enter the shantytown there were no rules or regulations to keep us from buying from the vendors who sold their wares along the road. I had told him about Grace.

I pointed her out and said, “That’s the little girl I was telling you about. She is beautiful, isn’t she?”

I opened the door of the car and walked over to Grace. This time she did not look startled and seemed as if she was expecting me.

I squatted in front of her and said, “Did you give Granny my message?”

This time she answered me. "Yes, Sergeant, I did."

"What did she say?" I asked.

"She told me that she was too busy to see you."

"What does your Granny do?" I asked.

"She washes and irons the Major's uniforms," she said.

"The Major's?" I said.

She nodded her head. There were only two Majors on the Base. One was Major Douds, my commanding officer, and the other Major Wilson who was an Adjutant to the Colonel. I knew that most of the officers had cleaning women and no doubt they also took care of their uniforms. Enlisted men had their laundry done by the Base laundry.

I said, "I will take two mangoes," and I had a ten-shilling note that in those days was worth about two dollars.

She looked at the note, and said, "I have no change, Sergeant."

"You take this and give it to Granny and then you can give me the change the next time I see you." Before I rose, I then said, "Where is your Mommy?"

She looked sad, and then with tears welling in her eyes she said, "I don't know. She went away."

"Does your Granny know where she is?"

"No, Granny doesn't know either."

I thought that was strange but there were many instances of mothers leaving their children with relatives while they were off seeking work elsewhere. I reached out, and patted her on the cheek and she shrank away. Poor timid soul, I thought. She was probably badly hurt. As I started to walk away I had an idea and I turned and went back.

"I have another message for your Granny. Will you give it to her for me?"

"Yes, Sergeant," she said.

"Ask her if she would do my uniforms."

"I will ask her, Sergeant," and she wiped away her tears.

I went back to the car and got in and we took off. On the way to May Pen I told McGuire that Father Kiely had seen her Granny and her in church. They had been missing for quite a number of weeks and he did not know what had happened to them. I told him that I was sure that there had been some trouble and that I could tell that she missed her Mommy wherever she was.

Several days later I glanced across the road and saw her there. I knew the MP on duty and he said to me, "Is that your girlfriend, Sarge?"

"Don't be smart. She is a poor lonely little girl and I want to help her out."

He said, "Don't go beyond the road or I will turn you in."

I shot back, "And the next time when I give you a shot I will use a dull needle."

He cringed and I walked across the road to where Grace was sitting and before I could speak she said, "My Granny said she would like to take care of your uniform Sergeant."

"That will be great. You wait here and I will go and get one and bring it back to you."

I walked back to the gate, the MP was busy examining the pass of a Jamaican worker. I went to my barracks and picked up a dirty uniform and put it in a paper bag and brought it back to Grace. I thought I may never see this again nor Grace but nothing ventured, nothing gained. She took the bag with the uniform, picked up her basket of mangoes and disappeared into the shantytown. I did not see her for two days and when I did spot her I walked over. She had a neatly wrapped package tied with a string and handed it to me.

"How much do I owe your Granny?" I asked.

She said, "Nothing. She owed you for the ten shilling note you gave me."

I did not offer her any money, as I did not want to create a situation between her and her grandmother. When I got back to my barracks and opened the package, my uniform was spotless and neatly pressed and folded. Well, I thought, if a Major can get his uniforms cleaned outside the Base laundry, so could I. There was no rule that I knew of that would be broken. For the next several weeks I brought my uniforms and would pick them up several days later. I did not mention to Major Douds anything about my transaction. Later I found out that it was Major Wilson whose housekeeper was friendly with Granny. The Major thought that his housekeeper was doing his uniforms.

One day Grace told me that her Granny wanted to see me. Maybe I would learn more about Grace.

"When will I see her?" I asked.

Grace looked around to see if anyone was listening and quietly said, "She told me that she can't meet you here but that on Sunday she would be under the big banyan tree on the road to May Pen."

"But what time?" I asked.

"She didn't tell me, Sergeant. She just said sometime in the afternoon."

"You tell her that I will be there."

I was surprised that she chose a banyan tree for I knew that many Jamaicans were frightened of the tree for it was supposed to be the residing place for spirits known as Duppies. The superstition handed down over the years came from what was known as the Ninth Night. It seemed that after a person was buried the spirits roamed the earth for nine nights. The relatives and friends and anyone from the village held a special ceremony. It lasted for nine nights and it consisted of singing, dancing to the beat of drums, and wailing throughout the entire night. The first few days were devoted to mournful songs, wailing and crying followed by nights of drinking, singing, clapping and wild dancing, joyfully leading the dead one to his resting place. Those who died with no one to conduct the Ninth Night ceremony, their spirits lived in the banyan tree and were known as Duppies. I surmised that Granny chose the banyan tree to afford us some privacy for most of the natives would make wide berth as they passed.

I looked forward to Sunday for I might unravel the mystery that surrounded Grace. I did not say anything to Father Kiely after Mass. I did not say that I was going to pedal to May Pen. I would see first what Granny had to say. In the early afternoon I hopped on the bike, left through the gate and headed toward May Pen. After biking for two miles I spotted in the distance the large banyan tree and as I approached I saw a lone woman sitting on her haunches beneath the tree. It always amazed me how the women could spend hours on their haunches instead of sitting directly on the ground. They were used to carrying heavy loads on their heads and had perfect posture. Another reason that I surmised for not sitting was to avoid coming in contact with the crawling creatures that abounded everywhere. They were especially frightened of lizards no matter how small or how large. I found them fascinating. There were some that if you grabbed them by the tail, the tail would fall off. Others changed colors to suit the background. I was surprised when they extended a balloon-like structure under the chin that was usually a brightly colored red. This was used to attract insects and the mate. The cry sounded like a ghekko. They were everywhere, in our barracks, mess halls and even in the chapel. They were a wonderful distraction especially during a boring sermon. The Jamaicans when seeing one would scramble, shouting, “Dem debbils dem!”

I laid my bike on the grass and approached Granny who rose when she saw me. She was a tall, slim, erect woman, dressed in an immaculate cotton dress. A yellow silk bandana was wound around her head under which one could glimpse gray hair. Her brown face was creased with wrinkles. Her gray eyes were a stark contrast. Drooping from her mouth was a white clay pipe with wisps of smoke curling from the bowl. She had on black low heel shoes that I knew were worn only for special occasions. Most of the time they went barefooted. I approached her and held out my hand but she did not take it.

I said, "Are you Granny? I'm Sergeant Crouch."

"I know you, Sergeant Crouch. I have seen you talking to my Grace."

She had spread a colorful straw mat on the ground and told me to sit. She had a small basket that I could see was filled with fruit. She had a small machete, a deadly instrument that could be used productively for such chores as chopping sugar cane, bananas or the like or a deadly weapon as a means of protection. I was sure that she used it for both reasons. She lifted a coconut and with one swipe chopped off one end and offered it to me. When I had first tasted coconut milk I did not like it, but on my long bike rides I had learned that it was a refreshing drink and I accepted it and thanked her. I took a long drink. Then she offered me a banana, which I declined.

I said, "I will have that later. Thank you, Granny."

"You have been very good to my grandchild, Grace, and I am grateful to you, Sergeant. She is very shy and lonely," she said.

"That I know, Granny. It was hard for her to even talk to me and once when I reached out to touch her, she drew back."

Granny looked at me for a few moments and then said, "Everyone in our village call you the Leper Sergeant."

I was startled. "Why do they call me that?"

"They know that you have visited the leper colony in Spanish Town. When they found out that I was washing your clothes many of the women avoided me."

I said, "But leprosy cannot be spread through clothing or even by shaking hands."

"I don't believe that." She shook her head. "That is why I told Grace not to let you touch her."

Things were beginning to clear up.

She puffed on her pipe for a few seconds. "I trust you, Sergeant, and that is why I asked to see you for I want you to do something for me."

"If I can, Granny, I will. You can be sure of that."

"I want you to take a letter to someone in the leper home."

"I don't know when I will be visiting next but I will be glad to do so. Who is it for?" I asked.

She looked down and softly said, "My daughter."

I was stunned. The pieces of the puzzle were falling into place.

"Grace's mother?" I asked. She nodded her head. "Does Grace know her mother is there?"

"No, I have never told her and I am very fearful that she might find out. If she did she would run away and try to reach her mother. That is why you must promise me that you will never tell her."

"You have my promise, Granny." I took another sip of the coconut milk. "I should not ask you this but could you tell me how your daughter got leprosy?"

She sat down on the mat, took the pipe out of her mouth and emptied the bowl onto the ground. "It is a long story and I know you want to get to May Pen."

"No, Granny," I said. "I have all afternoon. I will get to May Pen and if you trust me I would be very interested in hearing your story for I am sure that I could help both you and Grace."

"You are a good man, Sergeant. I could tell because of your concern for Grace." She straightened out her dress. "I suppose that I should start at the beginning."

"My parents had arrived in Jamaica from Haiti aboard a fishing vessel, landing at night at a beach near St. Anne's Bay in Ocho Rios. They had no papers but were taken in by the inhabitants of a village consisting of grass huts and cabins on the outskirts of St. Ann's near a sugarcane plantation. No one asked any questions despite their accent and they easily obtained work on the plantation as field hands. Eventually my mother gave birth to three children, two boys and a girl whom she named Bernadette."

Granny interrupted her story to say, "That's me."

She continued. "They were devout Catholics, which set them apart from most of the other workers. The loose living of all in the shantytown disturbed them but they desperately needed work. When I was seven I joined my mother, father and two brothers working in the fields. I was too young to cut cane so I was given the task of separating the good stalks from those that had rotted. An Englishman, Sir Richard Snowden and his wife, Lady Snowden, owned the plantation. They lived in the Great House surrounded by green lawns and English gardens. On the property was a building that housed the servants. Another was a stable with six spirited purebred horses. They had a teen-aged daughter, Lady Catherine, who lived with them and a son named Malcolm, who was in school in London. The workers saw little of the owners and their family. The plantation was divided into sections. An overseer, a black Jamaican, well built and domineering, supervised each section. They often used a whip to beat those whom they considered indolent, not pulling their fair share. The workers hated the overseers. It was not strange that some overseers did not show up for work because the workers wielded large sharp edged machetes to cut the cane. They never discovered their bodies because they were hacked to death, the parts tossed to the sharks that constantly patrolled the sea. Another man just as mean-spirited soon replaced them." Granny picked up her small machete. She looked at me with a strange smile and with one swipe of the blade cut off the top of a coconut, lifted it to her lips and took a long drink. I was sure that in case of trouble she could take care of herself.

"One day there was much excitement as the owner's son Malcolm arrived. He was a well-built handsome young man with curly blond hair and hazel eyes. He dressed in riding clothes; a white shirt with ruffles in the front, riding breeches, and boots and always carried a riding whip. He galloped around the plantation on a big black horse. Both the rider and the horse had wild streaks in them. His father placed him in charge of the plantation. He fell victim to the demon, rum. He visited my section of the plantation frequently and it was not long before my mother realized what was happening and drew me closer to her.

"One day a servant from the Great House arrived and said something to the overseer who pointed to my mother. The servant told my mother that Lady Snowden wanted to see her in the Great House. My mother wanted to refuse but knew that she couldn't and followed the servant past the huge boiler house with a tall chimney spewing out smoke. It was there that the sugarcane was refined and beyond that another brick building where sugar was distilled into rum. My mother hoped that she was going to be transferred to either of these buildings where her pay would be increased. My mother entered the Great House. It was the first time that she had ever been in such a splendid establishment. She had entered the kitchen where the servants eyed her coldly because 'house people,' the old caste system at work, never accepted the 'yard people.' Her clothes were stained and sweaty from the hard labor and she felt uncomfortable. Soon a short stout woman dressed in a black dress with a white collar and white cuffs on her sleeves, entered the kitchen and told my mother to follow her. She was Mrs. Hennessy, a light skinned Jamaican woman whose ancestors came from Ireland. She sat in a chair in a small parlor while my mother stood near her. She said that she was the housekeeper, which was the highest-ranking female servant in the Great House. Mrs. Hennessy was in charge of all of the other servants. She told my mother that Lady Snowden had heard of her sewing ability and wanted her to come and work in the Great House as a seamstress. Her wages would be doubled. My mother thought of all of the things that she could buy her family but then remembered quickly that she would be leaving me alone in the fields, which was not a good idea with Malcolm prowling about. She knew that if she refused she would be fired as well as my father, my two brothers and me. Once word got around to the different plantations they would never find work there again. But I came first and my mother told the housekeeper that she could not do that unless her daughter came with her. The housekeeper, sensing the pride and stubbornness in my mother, said that there would be a job in the kitchen for me assisting the cooks. With this my mother agreed. The housekeeper told her that we would be provided with uniforms and that we must bathe every day. That night in the hut my mother told us the good news. Everyone was excited, especially my father, who was happy that his wife would no longer have to engage in back-breaking labor and it would be a chance for his daughter to climb the ladder to newer and better positions. Another condition of employment insisted on by my mother was that we would not live in the servant quarters but would return to our hut at the end of each day's work. This was agreed to provided that we did not take our uniforms with us. My mother became suspicious. Why were they giving into her demands? All they really had to do was to command her to obey. There must be a reason, she thought, but she erased her doubts since she would now be better able to provide for her family.

"Everything went smoothly for the first few weeks. The kitchen staff accepted me when they saw me in my uniform. They thought I was a beautiful girl and well educated. I spent my days in the kitchen, peeling vegetables, washing pots and pans and never got to see the other parts of the house as there were different servants for different chores and those who served the meals were young men dressed in white coats. My mother was given a small room with several sewing machines next to the laundry. She was happy for she was doing work that she loved.

"The door opened and Malcolm entered, dressed in khaki riding breeches, carrying a crop. He ordered one of the servants to fetch him a glass of rum punch. He received the glass and downed the punch in several long gulps. As he was leaving the kitchen, he spied me, and after a few moments asked if I would like to see the horses. I was deathly afraid of these large animals, but fearing him more, I left with him, as many of the servants turned their heads. As we entered the stable, the horses were kicking in the stalls and snorting which frightened me even more. Taking a piece of carrot, he showed me how to hold it in my open hand and led me to one of the horses. I could not resist as he held my trembling hand under the horse's mouth. I was amazed at the gentleness of the horse as he took the carrot with his soft lips from my shaking hand. Then Malcolm lifted me up and put me on a seat of an empty carriage and showed me how to hold the reins. I lost much of my nervousness, since he was so kind to me. Suddenly, he lifted me up and threw me down on the straw covering the floor. He tore at my clothes and was on top of me. Frightened and confused, I screamed out but he held his hand over my mouth and threatened me that if I told my mother or anyone what had happened, he would kill us all."

Granny sobbed, jumped up and ran to the banyan tree. As she approached the tree, a flock of shrieking vultures, "birds of death," rose from the branches. I turned my head and fought an impulse to get on my bike and ride back to the Base, but I could not leave Granny in that condition. I wanted to put my arms around her, but realized she wanted to be alone as she relived that episode of horror. I turned my head away from the tree and watched the road, with her wracks of sobbing ringing in my ears. Soon the sobbing stopped, and she came back and sat down beside me. The tears on her dark cheeks glistened in the sunlight.

She said, "I am sorry, Sergeant."

I held her hands and said, "Don't be sorry, Granny. It is not necessary that you continue."

"No, no, Sergeant. I am all right, I want to tell it all." So she continued her story.

"When he left, I gathered my clothes, sobbing uncontrollably. The horses stumped in their stalls hearing my wailing sounds but no one came to my rescue. The stable hands moved further away from the building. They knew what had happened but could do nothing. After I dressed and wiped my eyes, my first thought was to run away but I knew that they would find me and kill my parents and my brothers so I went back into the kitchen. When the staff saw my rumpled dress and tear-stained eyes they gasped and looked away. They too knew what had happened and did not want to get involved - all, that is, but Birdie, the chief cook, who was short and well built. Her skin was ebony black. On her head was a white bandana wound like a turban. Everyone loved her but feared her at the same time. She ran the kitchen her way and no one complained, not even the stern housekeeper as Birdie created miracles with the food that she prepared. She immediately came to me and took me into the pantry, smoothing my dress, and with her apron, wiped away my tears. She held me in her large arms and put my head on her ample breast and told me not to cry and to remain quiet. Birdie said everything would be all right. She then closed the door to the pantry and holding me by the shoulders told me in a hoarse whisper, that I should sit there and be quiet and she would get my mommy.

"She soon returned with my mother who was shaking and frightened. Once again she closed the door and firmly told my mother to listen and do as she told her and everything would be all right. If she didn't we would be in big trouble. She said that Mr. Malcolm was a mean man and she could not fight him. The law would be on his side. If she told anyone, even her husband or her sons, and if they challenge him, they would not have long to live and if they left the plantation he would have them hunted down until he found them. My mother and I were thoroughly frightened. Birdie then went on and told my mother to act as if nothing had happened and at the end of the day when she went home, she should pack my suitcase. Birdie asked my mother if she knew of her friend named Effie who lived near us. My mother nodded her head. Birdie took out a piece of paper and wrote down an address. She told my mother that Effie's daughter was married to a businessman and they lived in Kingston. They had three children. Birdie said she would get word to her to expect me. She assured my mother that they would take me in and give me loving care and if a baby came she would know what to do.

"I cried out, 'A baby, I'm going to have a baby?'

"Birdie told me to 'Sssh,' since we wouldn't know for several months and we couldn't take any chances. My mother said that she couldn't send her little girl away when I would need her. Birdie asked her what good she would be to me if we were all dead. She continued to tell my mother that she didn't know the ways of this country. If Mr. Malcolm sees her, her husband and sons working without me, he would not make trouble. He would just assume that they had accepted what had happened. She told my mother that after a while, if she wished, she could leave the plantation and go to Kingston to be with me but not then, not for several weeks.

"My mother, protector of all of her family, knew that she would do as Birdie suggested. When we arrived back in our hut that evening, my mother tried to act as if nothing was the matter. My father, noticing that I was quiet, asked my mother what was troubling me and my mother told him that I was not feeling well. My mother said that I was having women's trouble and Birdie, the cook, suggested that I should visit her friend in Kingston for a few weeks until I was feeling better.

"When all of the rest had gone to bed my mother packed my straw suitcase and took me over to Effie's house where she was waiting for her. Effie told me that there was a truck with bags of sugar leaving at three in the morning. She knew the driver and he would take me to Kingston. My mother gave me the note with the name of Birdie's friend in Kingston, held me close for a long time and said that I shouldn't worry and that she would see me soon.

"Effie took me and my suitcase down to the road and we waited until we saw the headlights of a truck that came to a stop. When the driver saw Effie and me, he told me to get into the back and to hide between the bags of sugar. Effie kissed me and told me not to worry, Birdie knew what she was doing and I would be well taken care of.

"All I could do between my tears was to whisper, 'Thank you and God bless you.'

"I scrambled into the back of the truck and squeezed myself between the bags of sugar as it took off for Kingston."

CHAPTER SEVENTEEN

BERNADETTE TOOK OUT HER PIPE, filled the bowl and lit it. She offered me another coconut but I declined and took instead a ripe Bombay mango, peeled it and took big bites around the central pit. It was juicy and sweet. It was refreshing. I used my handkerchief to wipe my mouth.

"Life is so cruel. I don't know how you people keep from rising up in rebellion against these injustices," I said.

Granny chomped down on her pipe and said between her tight lips, "It's coming soon. That day is near." Then she took the pipe from her mouth and said brightly, "But that was more than 25 years ago, Sergeant, and things have improved since then but not much. We have our own ways of revenge."

When I asked her what she meant she just shook her head. "What happened to you when you arrived in Kingston?"

"Effie's daughter took me in. They were very kind and happy to have me, as I was able to watch their children while the two of them went to work. I did have a baby and they took good care of me. I had received word that my father had died of a heart attack while working in the fields. My two brothers signed on to a banana boat and I believe they are now in England. My mother lived with Effie for a while. She came to Kingston to be with me when my child was born. She was baptized and I named her Mary, since I loved the Mother of God so much."

She pulled out the silver chain around her neck revealing a Miraculous Medal attached. I was immediately struck with all of the pieces of the puzzle falling into place. This was no coincidence, I thought. This was the work of the Blessed Mother. Back in my barracks, in my footlocker, wrapped in a linen towel was the statue of Our Lady of Lourdes that I had rescued from an abandoned farmhouse during my teens. I carried it with me everywhere I went. I am usually a skeptic but I truly believed that Our Lady appeared to the peasant girl, Bernadette, in a cave at Masabielle, Lourdes, France and that it was no coincidence that I found that statue sitting alone in an empty farmhouse. It was meant for me. And here was Granny whose name was Bernadette who had conceived her child in the town of St. Ann's, name of the Blessed Virgin's Mother, and who had named her own child Mary, who named her child Grace. It was all fitting together. Hail Mary, Full of Grace. I knew that Our Lady was asking something of me. At that moment I did not know what it was but the puzzle was soon to be completed.

Granny continued. "I was afraid that Malcolm would find us and harm Mary and me. I prayed constantly. Then Effie's daughter received a letter from Birdie telling her that the Snowdens had sold the plantation and returned to England including Malcolm."

"My prayers were answered." She took out the Miraculous Medal that hung around her neck and kissed it. I knew that Grace was in good hands.

"My mother took care of my baby allowing me to seek work to support us. I had learned the skills of sewing and found a position as a seamstress in the Myrtle Bank Hotel. Effie's son-in-law built a small room onto his house allowing my mother, my child and me to continue to live with them. They shared their meals and I was able to pay Effie's daughter a small amount for room and board. Little Mary was a beautiful child. Her skin was light. Her hair was a soft brown color, her eyes large and brown with thick lashes. Her nose was perfectly formed and her lips full. She was a bright child and inquisitive. She wanted to learn everything. When she was five I enrolled her in the parish school, which was taught by Blue Nuns, a native order founded by a Dominican Nun. She was one of their brightest children. The Pastor of the church told me that with proper training my little girl could have a career in music. She had a beautiful voice and took easily to the piano. I did not know where I could get the money to afford such an education but Father Barry assured me that when Mary was twelve she would be able to enroll in a private girl's boarding school run by the Dominican Nuns. The nuns had been known to take in poor students who could not pay the full tuition. I would cover the room and board and he was sure that Mary would be eligible. Six months before Mary's 12th birthday, my mother died. Panic struck as I thought I would have to give up my job at the Myrtle Bank Hotel to care for my child. I had been putting aside a small amount each month to cover the room and board at the private boarding school. When I approached my boss, the hotel manager, to tell him that I would have to leave, he asked me why. I said I would have to be home when Mary came home from school. He did not want to lose me for I was an excellent worker and produced such fine results with my needle. He suggested that my daughter could come to the hotel after school and stay with me until my work was done. This arrangement worked out fine for not only did my daughter come to the hotel after school but also she helped me with the sewing for which we were given an evening meal from the restaurant kitchen. When my daughter was 12, I enrolled her in the convent school. Now I did not have to worry except on weekends when the students were allowed to go home and I arranged my hours so that I did not have to work from Saturday afternoon until Monday morning."

I was getting restless as I listened to Granny tell this sad tale, but I did not want to rush her for I knew she was relieving herself of a tremendous burden that she had kept hidden inside her for these many months and years, and so she continued.

"My daughter was accepted by all of the other girls in the private school despite the fact that they came from wealthy families. With her beauty, her talent and her ability to learn quickly, Mary soon became the leader of her class and often appeared in class plays and music recitals, which I attended. With the money I earned at the hotel and fulfilling requests for alterations and mending from all of my neighbors, I was able to afford the rental of a small cottage in Halfway Tree that was closer to the convent school."

"Everything seemed to be going great for you and Mary," I said.

She was silent for a while. "It was," she said and her finger made circles in the dirt, "and then all of a sudden all our dreams and hopes were dashed."

I looked over at Granny and said, "I know that you are getting tired. This must be exhausting for you. Do you want to stop now?" I still did not know how her daughter was sent to the Leprosarium but it could wait.

Granny heaved a deep sigh then braced her shoulders and said, "No, Sergeant, I want to finish for I need your help."

As she continued her story I did not ask many questions, as I wanted to get back to the Base. It had been more than two hours since I left.

Granny then told me that Mary graduated with honors and had many offers of employment. "I was hoping that she would become a teacher but then I found out that my daughter had a secret hidden life." Granny fingered her medal. "She was always such an obedient girl. I never caught her in a lie but during the last years of her schooling she would often go out at night telling me that she was going to a party at the home of one of her classmates. I trusted her. Never questioned her but she had a wild streak in her. No doubt from her father. She was meeting boys and going to bars. She took up with a drummer in a Jamaican band and became their lead singer. It was then that she told me that she wanted a career in the entertainment world and wanted to be a movie star. I was heartsick, but there was nothing that I could do for Mary, since she was now 17. I felt that it was during these years that she became infected with leprosy.

"A new nightclub was opening up. A couple from Chicago owned it. The club promised to be the tourist attraction of the islands. It was named the Glass Bucket. A young man had accompanied the owners from Chicago and he was a musician and he formed a first class jazz band. He was producing a floorshow for the nightclub. My daughter, Mary, heard about it through one of the band members. She auditioned and was hired on the spot for she was beautiful and had an outstanding voice. The American paid well and in addition to her salary she was given a percentage of any drinks she could coax the customers into buying. She visited the tables at which only men sat. They were usually soldiers or members of the business community. There was a dramatic transformation in her. She began to wear provocative clothing and heavy make-up. One day I noticed a change in Mary. She was showing symptoms of pregnancy. The day came when she could no longer hide it and had to leave her job at the Glass Bucket and once again I was caring for her. Despite my protestations she did not want to go to the doctor. She never left the house and I delivered the baby. It was a beautiful little girl and Mary named her daughter Grace. She had stopped going to Mass and the baby was not baptized. Not long after the birth of Grace, Mary noticed a skin rash, which did not seem to go away and finally she went to the doctor. After many tests he gave her the horrible news that she had the first stages of leprosy and would have to be confined to the leper colony in Spanish Town. The doctor asked her if she had any relatives and Mary said no. She did not tell him that she had a baby or that she was living with me, for she knew that we would become suspects and might have to be sent away as well.

"When she broke the news to me that night there was much wailing and weeping. Mary had to report to the Health Department the next day or the police would come and get her. I would have to take the baby and once again Effie's daughter came to the rescue. I questioned her as to who the father might be and she told me that she had relations with a Canadian officer in the Air Force who had been assigned to the Jamaican Army training pilots. I had no way of knowing whether this was true or not and just accepted her explanation. It was too late to do anything anyway and I began to blame myself for not keeping a closer eye over her.

"That was the last time that I saw Mary. I left my job at the Myrtle Bank without giving notice. I was now a fugitive. I could not stay in Kingston. They would eventually find me. I could not go back to St. Ann's for they would trace me there. Spanish Town was out of the question. I finally settled in May Pen where Effie knew a Chinese businessman who offered me a job as a housekeeper. He was very kind and allowed me to keep Grace at my side while I did my chores. At night we slept in a little shack at the back of the property and were given all of our meals. Occasionally, I would attend Mass at Father Kiely's church but I always made sure that I slipped into the pew after he had entered the altar and left before he had completed the last prayers. Grace was now approaching her fifth birthday, when I found out about the engineers building an Army Base not far in Sandy Gully. Word got to me that they were hiring workers. May Pen was filling up with many Jamaican Government Officials with the press in attendance which frightened me. So, I fled to the shantytown outside of the Army Base where I felt safer." Granny stopped talking. There was silence between us for several minutes.

She looked at me and said, "Well, that's it, Sergeant. That is my story."

I could not speak. It had been a long and emotionally draining day. The sun was beginning to set in the West, casting a reddish glow over the landscape.

Granny held her pipe in her hand and said, "All I want, Sergeant, is for you to let my Mary know that Grace and I are alive and that we miss her."

I was wondering how Granny would get back to her hut. A small cart pulled by a bedraggled donkey stopped on the opposite side of the road. Holding the reins was a large woman with a straw hat on top of her head.

Granny must have sensed what I was thinking and said, "That is my friend. She will take me home."

I stood up and hugged her, much to her surprise as she shrank back at my touch. "I will contact you," I said, "when I get any news."

She nodded her head. I jumped on my bike and started to pedal back to the Base. My mind was awhirl with ideas and plans on how I would bring about a reunion between two mothers and two daughters. There were many obstacles, so I took my Mom's advice and placed everything in God's hands. My Mom always told us that when we were confronted with a problem to try the best we could to solve it, and when we couldn't to let go and place it entirely in God's hands. She also told us not to stand over His shoulder telling Him what to do, as He does not like that. He will give you the strength to accept His will. Giving God my problems, I started to whistle as I pedaled down the dusty road finally arriving at the entrance to the Base.

CHAPTER EIGHTEEN

I ARRIVED BACK AT THE BASE FOR EVENING chow. No one asked where I had been. I was exhausted both mentally and physically. I looked forward to flopping on my bunk but I went to the operating room to check the schedule. There were no operations scheduled for the next day. Most of our operations were emergencies but Major Douds was an Ear, Nose, and Throat Specialist and scheduled as many tonsillectomies as he could to keep up with his practice. I made sure that I never showed any sign of a sore throat when I was around him. Lying on my bunk I was soon fast asleep and when I woke up moonlight flooded my room. It was almost midnight. I now had my own private room in the barracks, as did the other two Sergeants. I went to my footlocker and removed the statue of Our Lady and went back to my cot, slipping under the mosquito netting but sleep would not come. The sound 'ghekko' from a lizard, the buzz of the mosquitoes trying desperately to get through the netting that wanted my blood were all sounds of a tropical night, now familiar to me. There was the faint sounds of drums beating across the road in shantytown, the barking of a dog, and the cool breeze coming down from the mountains carrying with it familiar smells of burning wood mixed with that of honeysuckle. Now and then I heard a reconnaissance plane taking off on night patrol and another returning. My mind was a salmagundi of thoughts. I could not figure out the exact sequence of all that Granny had told me, especially about the Canadian pilot. Grace was now going on six and this was 1942 so she must have been born in 1936. Germany had not declared war until 1939, so what was a Canadian Air Force pilot doing in Jamaica training Jamaican pilots. I thought had Mary told her mother the truth about the father of her child and on and on my questions went.

Finally I said to myself, "That's all in the past, forget it. It is the present that counts and the future." I gripped the statue firmly in my hand and said, "Help me, dear Blessed Mother, to do the right thing. I am all that Grace and Granny have at the moment," and I fell asleep.

It was almost a month since I had talked to Granny before I made my next visit to the Leprosarium. Once again Father Kiely drove me, leaving me off at the gates and promising to pick me up when he returned from Kingston in three hours. Mother Mark was visiting a convent in Spanish Town so I had the wonderful opportunity of spending the time with Sister Mary Zita. She was a delight. She was in her early 40's but had the complexion and drive of a woman half her age. Mother Mary Mark was only temporarily assigned to the Jamaican Leprosarium, awaiting the day when the war would be over and she could take her place at the Mother General's Council in France. It was Sister Zita who was in essence the power behind the throne. It was she who bargained with the government, knew how to cut the red tape to get what she needed for the patients. There was a remarkable difference in the physical appearance of the Leprosarium in the short time since she had arrived there. New buildings had replaced most of the old dormitories. At present she was working on the new building to serve as an auditorium replacing the old recreational hall. The men were hard at work cutting brush and planting grass for a new sports area that would contain tennis and volleyball courts, a cricket and soccer field and a track for running races. She knew that activity was necessary to pass the many hours that the patients were confined to the Leprosarium, which led to boredom, which led to trouble. Both she and Mother Mark had a goal to start a school but they could spare no one from the small staff who worked tirelessly in caring for the medical needs of the patients. There was word from the Marist Headquarters in Bedford, Massachusetts that Carville, Louisiana. would be experimenting with the new sulfone drug Promin, but it was not yet available since it was still being tested.

At least there was a glimmer of hope on the horizon. I knew that Sister Mary Zita, having the responsibility of establishing and maintaining good relations with the Jamaican Government, would uphold the rules and I could not discuss my problem about Granny and Grace. I did skirt the issue by asking how the children were doing.

"They still have their dolls and toys that you brought at Christmas and they are constantly asking for ice cream." Her laughter had the lilt of the Irish.

"Is one of the Sisters in charge of the children?" I asked.

"Yes," she replied. "Sister Michael is in charge but she has two excellent women as assistants."

Could one of them be Mary? I thought. "Do the women have leprosy?"

"Yes, one has been here many years and her leprosy has been in remission. The other is a more recent arrival with the beginning stages of leprosy. She is a great help to us for she loves children. She plays the piano and has a beautiful voice."

It had to be Mary, I thought. How could I get a message to her? I did not want any of the Sisters to know that I had any connection, for if they found out that she had a child they would have to report that to the authorities. Sister solved the problem by asking me if I would like to visit the house where the children resided.

I jumped at the chance and I said, “Yes, I would, Sister. I would like to see them.”

We went first to the office and laboratory where I put on the long white gown and Sister took me to a part of the women’s Compound that had been fenced off. In the middle stood a two story wooden building. There was a small play area in the back with several large inflated colored balls resting on the lawn. Two girls were playing jacks. A little boy, no more than five, was pulling a little wagon and two other girls were playing with dolls. An elderly black woman who bore the scars of leprosy was sitting on a bench with a little girl and a boy on either side of her. She was reading from a book. I could hear the sound of the piano coming from inside the first floor. Mary, I said to myself. There were fifteen children living here from the ages of five to twelve. Two boys around the age of eight were kicking a soccer ball.

They looked up when they saw me and said, “Hello, Sergeant.” I was pleased they remembered me. I joined in their game of kick ball to their squeals of delight.

Then I said to Sister, “Is that a patient playing the piano?”

Sister Zita said, “Yes, doesn’t it sound lovely.” I nodded. “I would introduce her to you but she is very shy and would flee. She refuses to have anything to do with visitors. When you all came at Christmas she stayed in the house and would not take part in any of the activities. Unlike most of our patients, she is well educated. She is beautiful.”

“Is her leprosy far gone?” I asked.

Sister Zita shook her head. “No, fortunately it has not progressed much since she came here but that is not unusual for it takes many years in some cases for the leprosy to become full-blown.” We were strolling now back to the office. “Mary is a strange girl. She is one of the few Catholics here. Most of the others have converted since we arrived.”

I was delighted, for Sister Zita had given a name to the woman at the piano. It was Mary. Father arrived right on the dot. On the way back to the Base he told me that we would be receiving a new Army Chaplain, a Redemptorist, by the name of Father Daly.

"Does that mean you won't be seeing much of us at the Base?" I asked.

He laughed. "Aren't you happy I won't be looking over your shoulder. I know I am, for I have neglected much of my duties for my flock." He lit up another cigarette. "You know that my door is always open and it would be good exercise for you to bike over from the Base."

"We get plenty of exercise. Captain Effler is a Physical Ed nut. Without warning, he will call us to line up with a full field pack that weighs about 20 pounds and we are off on a 20–mile hike. Much as I would have liked, I never have dropped out. My pride keeps me going." He suddenly swerved to avoid hitting a goat. After I righted myself, having jammed up against the door I said, "Do you need new glasses, Father?"

"Don't be smart," he said. "I saw the goat. I just wanted to shake you up a little."

"Yeah," I said.

When I got back to the Base I printed a note, which I brought across the road to Grace who had a bundle of uniforms for me. I paid her and told her to give the note to her Granny.

The note read, 'I have seen Mary but I did not have a chance to talk to her. She looks well and is taking care of the children. I will get a message to her when I can, signed Sergeant.'

CHAPTER NINETEEN

SEVERAL WEEKS LATER THERE WERE changes at the Base. The new Army Chaplain, Father Daly, was short, very thin, had black hair and wore glasses. He was very different from Father Kiely. Father Daly was pleasant enough but quiet and aloof and adhered strictly to the rules. Back at May Pen Father Kiely found many GI's lined up outside his confessional on a Saturday night. Major Douds was sent back to the States and was replaced by a Lieutenant Colonel Shelley. Colonel Shelley was the direct opposite of his predecessor, Major Douds. Douds was fastidious and reserved and the staff did not hold him in high regard. Colonel Shelley was a rough and tumble man as tough as nails but had a deep understanding of human nature. In addition, he was an excellent surgeon. We hit it off from the start and he scheduled me to assist him at most of his operations. He could curse and yell and hit my hand with a retractor if I was not paying attention. This was something that he could not do with the Army nurses. When he found out about my visits to the Leprosarium, I often found a package of syringes, bandages, and the like that he told me were surplus and would be thrown away and perhaps the Sisters could use them. He was not a Catholic but was on the staff of a Catholic hospital. The Sisters at the hospital objected to his language in the operating room so he adopted the word sweetheart, which was a far cry from what he meant.

Occasionally, he would yell out "Sweetheart" to me in the operating room. This would cause subdued laughter. Then he would catch himself and roar, "You know damn well what I mean."

It was in the middle of September that I had my next chance to visit the Leprosarium to be met by a surprise. Two weeks earlier a new Sister had arrived by the name of Sister Mary Augustine.

When Mother had assembled all of the patients to introduce her, she started off by saying; "I have a surprise for you."

From that day on Sister Augustine was called Sister Surprise. First of all, it was easier than saying Augustine but secondly, she was a continual surprise to all of them as she revealed her talents, which were many. She was a convert and had entered her order in her middle 20's, which was considered old in comparison to the younger girls, many of whom had entered in high school. She had worked in the government offices in Washington, D.C. Sister was interested in the rough and tumble world of politics and knew how to handle red tape. She was outgoing, some would say forward. She did not fool easily. She was feared but respected. The men in particular were impressed for they had never seen a woman wield a hammer, saw, or paintbrush as Sister could. One of the reasons that she had entered the Marist Sisters was so that she could work in the leprosy colony. She wanted to do heroic things. Sister Zita told me that Sister Augustine's spiritual advisor, Father Kelly, had warned her that she would have to learn how to control her temper and to accept blind obedience.

After we met, Sister Mary Augustine, said to me, "Sister Zita told me that you are not one who makes a quick visit and never returns like so many others. I think we will get along."

Our friendship lasted for more than 50 years until her death in 1995. Fifty years of arguments and disagreements as both our iron wills clashed with one another. But fifty years also of love, confidence, respect and loyalty. After we shook hands on that day in September of 1942, I had a feeling that this was one Sister that I could have confidence in and would understand my situation with Grace and Granny. She was given the monumental task of starting a school for the children. She told me that one of the reasons that she had not entered a teaching order was that she did not wish to spend her life in the classroom. She was looking for action but God works in mysterious ways for she had no sooner arrived at the Leprosarium than Mother told her that she was to fill a dream of the Sisters to provide the children with an education. It would be difficult since the ages ranged from five years to fifteen years, most of them never having been in a school. She had to learn their customs, their medical condition, their lingo and discipline. They did not even have a schoolroom to begin with so they would have to use the chapel until a school could be built. There were no supplies or equipment, and little desire on the part of the children to spend hours in the school. This was the challenge she was looking for. She had gone to Spanish Town with Mother to buy whatever they possibly could in the way of crayons, paper, pencils, and slates. Classes began two days after she had arrived. After our introduction she excused herself by saying that she was too busy to have time to chat. No beating around the bush there. I knew immediately that I had found an ally in my quest to bring about a meeting between Grace and her mother.

The opportunity came a month later when I went to the Leprosarium to discuss the upcoming Christmas party, which was to become an annual event as long as I was in Jamaica. Sister Mary Zita had assigned her to work with me on the plans. Sister Augustine quickly recognized the spark between us. When we met in the parlor of the Convent she wasted no time in outlining the plans for the day.

When I told her that my mother and her group were willing to do the shopping for the gifts for each patient she said, "Why not let the Sisters do that? They know the needs of each patient, their likes and dislikes. Just give us the money and I will take care of it."

Just like that, I thought, the problem was solved. For now that we were at war, I knew that I would have a difficult time getting the gifts from New Jersey to Jamaica. I knew that Mom would be disappointed but would understand, and she immediately set about with bake sales, card parties and other activities to raise funds. She collected over a thousand dollars, which meant that each of the patients would have at least $5.00 for a gift. The soldiers at the Base would raise the balance for the refreshments. Later on Sister admitted that she did not realize what a tremendous task she had undertaken, and had to revise her list several times since she found out that much of what she wanted was not available in Kingston.

After we had a cup of tea and cookies and we were alone, the rest of the Sisters having gone to the Compound, I took a deep breath and said, "Sister, are you aware of the rules and regulations set by the Government on how to handle anyone with symptoms of leprosy?"

She smiled at me as if to say what a foolish question. "Of course," she said. "I studied everything I could get my hands on about leprosy before I even entered the Convent."

"I know, Sister," I said. "I mean the Jamaican rules from the Government."

She looked exasperated. "Sergeant," she said, "everyone is informed about their mission. I know the whole history of this place. How the patients got here, why they must stay here and all of the rules of isolation."

That's it, I thought. She would not understand and she would be the last one to help me.

Then she looked at me and smiled. "Have you broken any rules in the Army?"

I reddened, "A few."

"Well, there were many rules and regulations in the Convent which I did not agree with. Some did not make any sense."

"What did you do about that?" I asked.

She grinned broadly. "I broke a few too, but I had to pay for it."

"How?" I asked.

She looked at her hands. "I had to spend hours on my hands and knees, either scrubbing the floor or, worse still, emptying the grease traps under the sink." She laughed. "I had to pay for my transgressions, but I also had the satisfaction of expressing my disapproval of a stupid rule."

I laughed. "You must have been a problem to your Superiors just like I am to mine."

Just then a tiny green lizard skittered across the back of her chair. She didn't flinch and held out her hand hoping the lizard would crawl on it, but like me he just wasn't ready to trust her.

"Just ask Mother Mary Mark. She was my Superior when I was a Novice." The lizard jumped from the chair to the floor and disappeared.

"You are not afraid of them Sister," I said.

"I love animals, all kinds. I love them better than some humans." I'm sure she did, I thought.

"What about scorpions?" I asked.

"I'm not stupid," she sharply retorted.

My mind was changed now. There was hope here. I thought I would plunge in.

"What do you think about the segregation rules, Sister? Don't you think it is a cruel way to handle people who are just sick?"

"It is fear," she said. "Just fear. They don't know how you get the disease, they don't know how to treat it and so they take the easy way out and just keep them locked up. The most difficult job we have here is the fact that they are isolated with no hope. They are shunned today as in the time of Christ but there are laws and they must be obeyed until we find a better answer."

"But you just said that there are some laws that need to be broken," I said.

She looked at me sharply now. "What's on your mind, Sergeant? Spit it out. I know that you are leading up to something."

I reached for a cookie. There was a few seconds of silence. "I don't know you well but there is something about you that makes me trust you."

She reached out and touched the back of my hand. "Try me," she said.

There was no turning back now so I said, "Sister, I have something confidential to tell you but if you tell anyone it will ruin the life of a little girl and her Granny." I gulped.

"A little girl and her Granny," Sister said.

I swallowed and continued. "Her mother is a patient here."

Sister was quick to ask, "What's the patient's name?"

"Remember, Sister, I ask for your confidence."

She looked exasperated. "Let me judge that, Sergeant. What is the patient's name?"

"It's Mary, Sister. She is the young woman who works with the children."

Sister looked startled. "Mary? You mean the beautiful woman who sings so well and plays the piano?"

"Yes, Sister." There it was. I had done it and I hoped that I had not ruined Granny's or Grace's life.

Sister was silent for a moment. "That explains it," she said. "No wonder she is so silent and refuses to tell anything of her past life except that she used to work in a nightclub in Kingston. My, my," she said. "Poor soul."

"Granny told me that she is frightened," I said, "because if the authorities know that she has a child they will seek her out and possibly take the child for observation and maybe she will end up in the Leprosarium. At least that is what Granny is fearful of."

"Does Mary know that you know?" Sister said.

"No, I have never spoken to Mary. Whenever I come near she seems to disappear."

Sister thought a moment and said, "What are you asking me to do, Sergeant?"

"All that Granny asked me to do was to see if I could get a message to Mary to tell her that her little girl is doing well and not to worry."

Sister nodded her head and said, "That's no problem. I can do that. You just let me handle it. By the way how did you get to know Granny and Mary's daughter?"

"They live in the shanytown just across from the Base and Granny cleans my uniforms."

Sister stood up and looked through the screen on the porch towards the Compound. She turned back to me. "Mother will be wondering what is keeping us." I stood up and she walked over and took my hand. "Don't worry about a thing, Sergeant. If God wants it, it will all work out." She squeezed my hand. "You have my confidence. I will say nothing at the moment except to get your message to Mary. When will I see you again?"

"Colonel Shelley, the Chief Surgeon, is very good to me. He knows about Grace and her Granny and even examined them. He told me they have no signs of leprosy but we both know that the bacillus may lie dormant for years before manifesting itself." We left the Convent porch and headed towards the Compound. "I will try to get here sometime next week. I will tell him that we still have a lot to do to work out the details for Boxing Day."

She gave a short laugh. "It seems like we are birds of a feather, Sergeant."

I didn't know it then but we were birds of a feather. I affectionately always called her Sis and she called me Brudder.

After Father Kiely picked me up and we were driving back to May Pen I could not hide my enthusiasm.

"You look cheerful, Crouch," which he sometimes called me instead of Sergeant. "What happened at Spanish Town? Did you have too many beers?"

"You know I don't like beer, Father."

He flicked his cigarette. "Well it must be the old demon rum that's gotten you this way."

"Nope, wrong on both accounts. You will know soon enough when Sister Augustine works it all out for me," I said.

He looked at me. "Sister Augustine, heh. I have been hearing a lot about her lately."

I perked up. "Who has been talking?" I asked.

"My friend Father Sullivan, who is Pastor of Spanish Town and also has the Leprosarium as his responsibility."

I was a little worried. "What did you hear?" I said.

"I just met her today," he said. "She's a dynamo from all of the accounts that I have been hearing. She has turned the place around but she won't last long."

Again I worried. Would they send her home? "Why do you say that, Father?"

"Father Sullivan tells me that she is very argumentative. When she makes up her mind, that's it. Obedience is the path to sanctity."

I looked at him askance, "Always?"

"There you go again. You like an argument yourself," he said.

"Well, in the Army we are told to obey orders but we do have an out. We can question the order but we must obey first. Then we can put in a complaint to higher authority," I answered.

Then he said, "If you do that you better ask for a transfer."

I laughed. "That's true. I would hate to work under a Commander who has it in for me but I am lucky. Colonel Shelley is willing to listen to opinions before he gives a final order, but they better make sense."

"He is my kind of man. We have had many good discussions. He is a blunt man and while not a member of our faith he respects what the Church is doing here in Jamaica and offered to give me any help I might need."

I turned in my seat and looked directly at him. "So you have met the Colonel. What does he say about me?"

He lit another cigarette. "What makes you think I would betray confidences? That's between us. So don't ask any more questions."

Ah ha! I thought. Maybe I can tell him about Grace and Granny after all but I will wait until after I hear from Sister Augustine to see what her plans are. Eventually, I did bring him into my confidence and he became part of the Boxing Day Plot.

CHAPTER TWENTY

WHEN I RETURNED TO THE BASE I wasted no time in getting word to Granny. That night while lying on my bunk reading an Agatha Christie mystery, I thought how devious her plots were. With what I was planning that could lead me to become a writer of mysteries. I laughed, another career to add to your list. Will your mind never stop?

I put out the light and while I was saying my prayers I whispered, "Thank you dear Blessed Mother. Whenever anyone fled to you for protection or asked for your intercession, you always answered them. You have opened the door today and a bright light has entered to show me the way to bring hope to Grace and Granny."

Sergeant McGuire drove me to Spanish Town the next week. Stationed in the Command Headquarters he had access to the motor pool and I called on him often for help. He was always happy to get away for a few hours anyway and he told the Colonel that he was in on the planning for the Boxing Day Party at the Leprosarium. I did not clue him in on what Sister Augustine was planning as I did not know myself but I thought that the fewer who knew about what we were doing, the better. When we arrived I told Sister Mary Zita that McGuire had not seen some of the new buildings so that I could have a few moments alone with Sister Augustine. I then asked her where Sister Augustine was and she told me that she would soon be coming up to the Convent for lunch as the morning session of school had just ended. I asked her how it was going.

Sister Zita replied, "Better than expected. In fact now Sister is having an afternoon session for the adults and already 12 have signed up. Isn't that wonderful? Also, Sister has relieved me of other duties, such as the farm. She is going to reorganize the farm. She is so full of ideas we can't keep up with her."

"They hit the nail on the head when they called her Sister Surprise," I said.

Sister laughed and took Sergeant McGuire down to the Compound. I saw Sister trudging up the path from the Compound. She waved as she walked by, went into the changing room and joined me in the parlor.

"I'm so glad you came," she said. "Will you have a sandwich with me?"

"Sure," I said.

"How about a tuna fish and a coke," she asked.

"I will have what you have, Sister."

"How about mongoose on rye?" she said laughingly.

"OK by me," I said, shuddering as I thought of fried mongoose.

She disappeared into the kitchen and came back carrying a tray with two tuna fish salad sandwiches and two cokes.

After we had finished eating I was waiting for her to say something when she got up and said, "Follow me," and we walked toward the gate. When she was satisfied that we were alone, she said, "I have great news for you."

"Really," I said, excited.

"Yes, I spoke to Mary. I told her how impressed I was with the way she handled children and wanted her to help me with my school. She was eager to help. When we were alone, I said, 'Mary, I know about Grace.' She looked startled and turned quickly and was ready to walk away when I grabbed her arm. I told her she could trust me and that no one would know what we were discussing. That seemed to calm her down a bit." Sister stopped to examine a hibiscus bush growing along the road and plucked off some dead flowers. "All that I told her was that you had been to see me and that you were in touch with her mother and daughter as they are living close to the Army Base. Mary just stood there and said nothing." Sister stopped to watch a brightly colored hummingbird hovering over a flower sipping its nectar. Sister continued, "Mary started to cry. I put my arms around her and told her not to worry, that her secret was safe with me." Sister stopped and turned to look at me. "Mary accepted what I said and wanted to know how her daughter was. I told her that you saw them often and that her mother was worried that she would be angry with her because she had not contacted her since she entered here. Mary understood immediately. She said, 'My mother is a clever woman. She knows that any mail that she sends me might be intercepted and could be traced back to where she was living.' Then Mary asked if Grace had missed her or talked about her. I told her that you said that Grace is always talking about her Mommy and that Granny had told her that you had gone away for awhile."

"And what did Mary say when you told her that?" I asked.

"She was so relieved to know that both Grace and her mother were well and was overjoyed when I told her that Grace missed her. She said that she was afraid that Grace had forgotten her or didn't love her." We both jumped back a little when a mongoose ran across our path into the bushes.

I laughed and said, "There goes our sandwich." Sister laughed heartedly and we continued to walk toward the gate. "I wish there was some way that Grace could see her mother," I said, "but I know that this is impossible."

Sister looked at me slyly and said, "It is not impossible."

I stopped walking and said, "You are kidding me. How can that happen?"

"Just leave it to me. I think that I can arrange it during the Boxing Day party. Of course, Grace cannot enter the Compound but if you could find a way somehow to bring Granny and Grace to the gate on that day I could figure something out."

I said, "You will be breaking the rules. What if you get caught?"

"I'm not breaking the rules, Sergeant. I am bending them a little. Grace will still not be able to come into the Compound for the law is still very strict about children visiting here. Of course, Granny can come at any time."

"Well, I will have a hard time convincing Granny to allow Grace to come here, even to the gate. But if you can solve the problem so can I."

She laughed, "Remember we are birds of a feather." We turned around to return back to the Convent. I reached into my pocket and pulled out a five-pound note, which at that time was about $25.00 in American money. I handed it to Sister and she said, "What's this for, hush money?"

"No, if it were I am sure you would want more than five pounds. I want you to do me a favor."

"Oh, Oh," she said, "Isn't what I am doing enough for you? Do you want everything?"

"If I could have everything I would want it. All that I want you to do is to buy the nicest doll that you can find when you go shopping to Kingston for the gifts. Then when I bring Grace, Mary can present it to her daughter as a gift from her."

"Good idea, Sergeant." She took the five-pound note and tucked it in her apron. "We would make a good team."

"Yeah," I said, "The Sergeant and the Nun." Forty years after that day we wrote our first book, authored by the Sergeant and the Nun.

Sister Zita and Sergeant McGuire were halfway up the path from the Compound when we met.

I said, "We have to get back to the Base."

McGuire looked startled as he was ready to spend the afternoon but he said nothing. We said our good-byes, got into the sedan and took off for the Base. On the way back, he asked if I had finalized all the arrangements with Sister Augustine and I told him that we had, never revealing what either of us had said. My mind was deep in thought as I pondered how I would get Granny to agree to bring Grace to the Leprosarium. But I brushed it off and thought that I would think about that tomorrow. Then McGuire said that he was planning for a trip to Ocho Rios to visit Shore Park Hotel and would I like to go along? I jumped at the chance. I got word to Granny that I wanted to see her at our usual meeting place under the banyan tree and she agreed.

The next few days in between my usual duties I kept thinking of how I was going to get Granny and Grace to Spanish Town. We could not ride in Army vehicles. There was no bus and finally I realized that the only one who could help me out was Father Kiely. I would have to tell him what we were planning to do and I hoped that he would go along. When I discussed everything with him he agreed that he would bring Granny and Grace in his car to the gate of the Leprosarium on Boxing Day. Now my job was to convince Granny. We met under the banyan tree. She offered me the usual coconut but I declined, as I was not thirsty. I explained everything to her of my contact with Sister Mary Augustine and that it would be possible for Grace and her mother to see each other. Granny looked frightened and doubtful but I assured her that Sister Augustine could be trusted and no one but Father Kiely, Sister Augustine and I would know anything about our plans.

When I had finished, she waited a long time before she answered and looked at me and said, "I trust you, Sergeant.

Grace and I owe you a lot and I know that you would not do anything to betray me, so tell me what I should do."

I then told her that I would find out what time on Boxing Day that she and Grace should be under the banyan tree and Father Kiely would pick them up there. Before she left she took my hand. The first time that she ever touched me.

Her gratitude overcame her fear and I said, "Granny, I wouldn't tell Grace. She will be all excited. She might blurt it out to others and if the plans had to be cancelled she would be broken-hearted."

Granny told me that she knew that I was right and that she would not say anything to Grace other than Father Kiely was going to take them for a ride. So the stage was set.

CHAPTER TWENTY-ONE

I RECEIVED A THREE-DAY PASS TO begin on the Friday after Thanksgiving through the weekend to go to Shore Park, thanks to Sergeant McGuire. Corporal Ray Fontana of the Infantry was to join us. The three of us left early Friday morning and headed northward toward Mt. Diablo, the devil's mountain, so called because of its steep and winding climb and its height. The road was bounded on one side by steep granite cliffs and on the other side by many precipices, fortunately protected by guardrails. They looked too flimsy for me to hold back a ton of metal. I would not travel this way by night, for one slip and over the precipice you would go. There were many hairpin turns and the views were spectacular. One could see below tiny little villages clinging to the sides of the mountain where there were several plateaus. There were green meadows. There were sheep and goat farms and many swiftly running streams rushing down the mountainside, creating spectacular waterfalls. When the sun's rays were correctly positioned, there were beautiful rainbows. You would then go for long distances with huge trees clinging to the sides of the mountain. The further up you went the cooler it became, and eventually we reached the town of Moneague. This area is known as the Upland Savannahs. Many of the wealthier people had summer homes here. Neat whitewashed cottages with lovely gardens. There were patches of strawberries and we stopped to purchase a basketful from one of the many roadside stands that dotted the way, selling all kinds of produce. We also bought a fresh pineapple, mangoes and for me a bottle of coke and for the two other guys Red Striped beer, which was manufactured on the island.

We drove out of town and stopped along the road, bordering a rapidly moving stream. The water bounding over the rocks formed little pools. We took off our shoes and dipped our feet in the ice-cold water. After first washing off the strawberries, the mangoes and the pineapple, we submerged the bottles of beer and coke in the cold water. McGuire took a small machete from the back of the trunk. I noticed that he knew how to use it. I wondered if he used it for utilitarian or defensive purposes. He cut the stem off the pineapple and sliced it down all sides into thick pieces. He had even brought paper plates and plastic forks and spoons. Being in the Quartermaster Corps had its advantages. He peeled the skin of the mango with his pocketknife and cut slivers of the pinkish, juicy flesh down to the middle pit. Between bites of strawberries, delicious sweet juicy pineapple, the mangoes, a long gulp of our drinks, and our feet turning blue, we had a wonderful picnic in the midst of spectacular scenery. I shut out thoughts of my fellow GI's on the hot sands of the Pacific Islands, facing a murderous enemy and on the other side living in crowded barracks all along the English coast preparing for the invasion of Europe. After we had our fill, we cleaned up. McGuire put all of the used paper plates and utensils in the bag, which he put in the back of the trunk. No littering here. No despoiling of this pristine beauty.

We took off again and after we left Moneague our route turned downward. Down and down we went, the air becoming warmer and warmer until we were at the base of the mountain, heading north. We could see the sea in the distance. We passed through a lane of tall bamboo, the tops of which bent over the road forming a natural arch for several hundred yards. It was cool here and on both banks of the road grew hundreds of different kinds of ferns. Some were tiny, others as tall as large bushes and small trees. It was named Fern Gully and was a botanist's delight. Coming out from the shade of the bamboo, the sun had reached its zenith and we began to breathe in the tangy smell of the sea. We soon came to a crossroad and turned onto a well-paved road that ran along the coast with waves crashing upon the rocks. The beautiful Caribbean shimmered with every color of the rainbow, depending on the depth of the water and the rays of the sun. On the other side were flatlands, containing many huts of all sizes and descriptions. There were parts of the coast that were hidden from the road, like clusters of tall coconut palms all bearing numbers on their trunks, which I found out later was their insurance number. They were all insured against the ravages of hurricanes. There also was a vast sugar plantation and I saw a sign ahead, St. Ann's Bay. My mind immediately flashed to Granny and Grace. Here is where Granny worked with her mother, father and brothers, cutting cane, and it was here where the saga, in which I was now involved, began with Malcolm taking advantage of Granny.

St. Ann's Bay is where Columbus first landed, where he spent more than a year due to illness, and where a monument stands commemorating that event. The town still bears the remnants of Spanish architecture. With the Spaniard's eye to create a new Seville, the coast was dotted with many coves and it was from one of these coves that the Spanish Governor of Jamaica fled by boat to Cuba when the English conquered the island. This was an area of the island known as Ocho Rios, the meeting of eight rivers and the garden of Jamaica. I was stunned by the beauty and let my eyes feast upon the palette of colors that greeted me.

Continuing our trip we heard the sound of roaring water and soon we viewed a spectacular falls on the side of the mountain. It was called the Roaring River Falls. At the base of the falls the water churned and foamed and ran in a rapidly moving stream into a series of smaller falls, cascading over rocks as it led to the sea. Unfortunately, while I was still in Jamaica, they harnessed most of the falls for electric power, destroying its beauty. But there is enough water to create rapidly moving cascades over descending ledges of rock into the sea. One can bathe in the Caribbean, then walk over to the falls for a luxurious cold shower to wash off the salt and if one is brave enough one can climb the falls, back to its source. The rocks are slippery in many places and if you lose your footing one can fall into a deep pool. We were to stay at the Shaw Park Hotel, a short distance away, and promised that we would take advantage of this unique spot.

Our car continued for a short distance. On one side of the road there were hills beyond which one could see the mountains. There was a driveway off the main road with a sign pointing to the top of one of the hills where the hotel was located. It was a short climb and at the top of this promontory we passed through gates over which hung the sign Shaw Park Hotel and entered a veritable paradise. The main building was modeled after a Swiss chalet with red tiled roofs. In addition to rooms in the main building, there was a line of cabana-like structures, which also contained individual bedrooms, all with verandas overlooking the Caribbean below. There was a tennis court, a cricket field and a riding stable. Attached to the main building was a long covered patio that served as the dining room, set with round tables, draped with white gleaming linens. In the center of each table was a crystal bowl of flowers, roses, wild orchids, blue delphiniums, purple and white irises. The table was set with fine china, crystal glasses and sparkling silverware. Wild canaries and parakeets darted in and out from under the roof. Another roofed building covered a gleaming wooden dance floor with a raised bandstand and a grand piano behind which was a covered, long mahogany bar, stacked with bottles of the finest liqueurs, scotch, rum, you name it. The most spectacular of all was the swimming pool that was fed from the stream at the base of a waterfall and left the pool in another waterfall cascading down to the sea.

If it weren't for the war, the lack of the wealthy tourists from Europe and the tight economy, no GI would ever be able to afford this luxurious retreat. However, the owner, whose name was Flora Stewart, an athletic English woman with white hair, a ruddy complexion and a winning smile, opened it to a select few of the GI's at one-tenth of the cost. Since it was mostly empty there were but a handful of servants, housemaids, waiters and a fabulous Swiss cook by the name of Paul who had gained a reputation as one of the finest cooks in the Caribbean. Flora had nabbed him on one of her trips to Switzerland when the hotel was filled to capacity. Her husband was a retired English Army Colonel and one seldom saw him except occasionally on the tennis courts. In its heyday they served the finest cuisine but now with the war and the import of foods from France and the Continent cut off, Paul created magical dishes from the local produce. Uniquely, in one of the small pools of water leading to the main swimming pool, Flora had her own crayfish pond, which were a delicacy. If it weren't for restrictions on travel and the laws forbidding currency to leave the island, Paul would have been long gone.

We chose to settle in three of the outside rooms. We were all willing to pay the extra cost to be alone for a few days after months of living in crowded barracks with no privacy. Each bedroom was tastefully furnished with a large bed covered with a large white chenille bedspread, heaps of luxurious pillows, covered by a canopy of mosquito netting. There were several end tables with lamps, white wicker armchairs with deep cushions covered with a fern leaf print fabric. There was an overhead ceiling fan but it was not necessary for we were near the mountains and between the breezes from the sea and the mountains one needed a blanket at night. The gleaming wooden floors were covered by oval mats, tightly woven of straw. On the veranda were several rocking chairs, small tables for drinks and canapés with the ever-darting canaries and parakeets searching for handouts. After shedding our uniforms and dressing in khaki shorts and a tee shirt we hurried to the bar and I ordered a frozen daiquiri. It tasted like nectar from the gods. We then changed into our bathing suits and went to the pool. The only way to get wet is to jump right in for if you go inch by inch you freeze to death. The pool was ice cold. To swim was refreshing.

We then changed back into our uniforms, as coat and tie were required for dinner. In the dining room there were two couples at one table and an elderly couple at another. That was it. It was eight p.m. and it was dark. The overhead Japanese lanterns glowed and there were lighted lampposts dotting the entire property. It was cool and several of the women in evening clothes wore shawls. There were hurricane lamps on each table and thankfully the canaries and parakeets had gone to sleep. The breeze kept down the insects and it was cool. There was only one waiter on duty. As soon as we entered he presented us with menus and filled our water glasses. Noticing our uniforms he said, "Ice?" and we all nodded. We were stamped as Americans. The first course, a delicious creamed mushroom soup with bits of ham. Then came a small crystal bowl filled with ice imbedded into which were six small red crayfish. They reminded me of prawns in New

Orleans. Their shells were thin and easy to crack. The small bits of meat, which tasted like crab, were hardly filling but delicious. Next came a piece of baked red salmon, covered with a delicious cream sauce sprinkled with chopped chives. A small dish with one scoop of tangy lemon sherbet to clear the palate followed this. The main course was a delicious rack of lamb, which the waiter carved on a small table. It was cooked to perfection. The center was a light pink. There was a faint smell of garlic and it had been seasoned with rosemary. On top of each chop was a sprig of fresh mint, small roast potatoes and a medley of vegetables. The dessert was a creamy, smooth chocolate mousse, sprinkled with shredded fresh coconut.

Then Flora Stewart invited us to join her for coffee in her private drawing room. She introduced us to her other guests. The distinguished looking English couple was Sir John Huggins, an aide to the Governor General of Jamaica and his wife, Lady Huggins. They were stiff and formal. The other two couples were Abe and Joe Issa and their wives. Their parents had come from Lebanon. I immediately recognized the name for I had seen it on the marquee of many of the stores in Kingston and Father Kiely had mentioned them. They were good Catholics and generous to the Church. Both boys had attended Boston College, run by the Jesuits. Joseph went onto complete Law School and had a thriving legal practice in Kingston. Abe kept to the business side of the family and was an entrepreneur in every sense, constantly juggling new ideas. Both wives were charming. The Huggins looked uncomfortable and I realized that the Issa's belonged to the merchant class. I, too, was wondering how Flora had become so intimate with them and during the course of the conversation the answer came loud and clear. The drawing room was comfortably furnished. Bookshelves lined the wall and were crammed filled with books. Large easy chairs covered in chintz, oriental rugs, and on the sideboard which was covered with a brocade cloth, stood a silver tray with two gleaming silver coffee pots, sugar and creamer and a three tiered cake dish filled with little cakes and cookies and several bottles of cordials and brandy. Everyone was invited to serve themselves. In our conversation I learned that Joe was well acquainted with Leonard Swaby and were often rivals in the courtroom. I told them of the delightful evening that I had spent at the Swaby's home in Kingston.

Abe said, "You have to visit us. We have a nice pool that you would enjoy."

I thanked him and said, "I may take you up on that."

I had several cups of the delicious Blue Mountain coffee. I skipped the pastries and ended with a snifter of brandy. Most of the conversations centered on the three of us, as they wanted to know everything that was going on at the Base. The two Issa wives said that they were signing up to work at the USO and I told them about Alice Mulally. Then Abe told us of his plans to build a first class hotel on the beach in Ocho Rios. There were a few small hotels and inns dotting along the coastline but nothing as spectacular as what Abe was planning. He was going to call it Tower Isle and was negotiating for the property. It would be open all year round instead of just the winter months unlike the other luxurious hotels. It would cater to the middle class. Flora did not say very much. I was sure she was thinking of the competition. If one traveled further northward there was the jewel of the Caribbean, Montego Bay, home for the rich and famous. There were two top hotels on the beach, one the Sunset Lodge that catered to the royal families of Europe and the ultra rich, and the other the Casablanca, a beautiful hotel adjacent to the famous Doctor's Cove. The water was so clear. One could see to a great depth and it was filled with colorful fish of every shape, size and color. Across from the beach was the Montego Beach Hotel catering to the business, professional and the upper middle class. I had yet to visit Montego Bay but was hoping one day to do so.

The Huggins soon bade us good night as did Flora and the rest of us went out to sit at the bar. There was a full moon creating a spectacular scene. Up and down the coast there were pinpoints of light from the cottages, huts and shacks. Out on the water could be seen the bobbing lights of fishing vessels. The tall coconut palms were silhouetted against the night sky. My two companions decided to take a walk. I think they were looking for more excitement but I was fascinated with the Issa's. An elderly Jamaican man in a white coat was tending bar. We sat on rattan armchairs around a table on which were bowls of potato chips, cashew nuts and peanuts, and a carving board on which were several cheeses and crackers. Abe told me of their friendship with Father Kiely and how sorry they were when he was transferred to May Pen from Kingston. I don't remember how the subject came up but I told them of my visits to the Spanish Town Leprosarium.

"Oh my," Mrs. Issa said. "How could you do that? Aren't you afraid of catching leprosy?" I told her of all that I knew and how difficult it was to contract it but she did not seem to be convinced.

Joe said, "I know Sister Mary Zita. I have helped her with some legal problems. She is really a go-getter."

He then told me of the opposition at first to the nuns taking over the Leprosarium, but Governor Richards, who had served in the South Pacific, was adamant. Joe admired the work that they were doing but he too had not visited the Leprosarium. They had young children and they did not want to expose them to the disease.

Abe then said, "Have you come across a young woman named Mary who is a patient?" My heart sank. What was I getting into? "She was a singer at the Glass Bucket Nightclub. She had a beautiful voice and knock-out looks." I could see that Abe had an eye for beautiful women.

"No, I haven't seen her when I visit there." I lied.

Joe spoke up, "She disappeared for awhile. No one knew where she had gone. We just assumed that she had run away with a member of the band but I found out later through my contacts with the health department that she had developed symptoms of leprosy and was admitted to Spanish Town."

Abe said, "So beautiful. I hate to think what the disease will do to her."

I kept silent. Joe was with the law and if he found out about Grace who knows what would have happened. I did not mention that Father Kiely was taking part in the little scheme I was hatching to bring Grace and her mother together. I changed the subject and talked of my love of the theatre, telling them of the plays and the musicals that I was in during high school and for a time after graduation.

"Do you play the piano?" asked Mrs. Issa.

"Only by ear. I never took any lessons."

Mrs. Issa said, "Why not play for us," pointing to the grand piano.

"Do you think that Flora would mind? Perhaps the noise would disturb them," I said, trying to get out of it.

"We are far from the main house and there aren't any guests. I'm sure that she wouldn't mind."

I got up and walked over to the piano. If I knew the tune, I was able to play reasonably well, hitting octave with my right hand and faking with the base. I was no Eddie Duchin, but I played well enough to be entertaining, although I had a difficult time with jazz so I kept to the ballads. I played several numbers by Noel Coward and Glenn Miller. When I finished they politely applauded and rose to go to their rooms. I was not a smash hit. We bade goodnight and the Issas told me that they were leaving early in the morning to return to Kingston. Joe gave me his address and told me not to forget to visit them. They would be delighted to have me. I walked over to the old bartender.

He said, "You sure can tickle the keys, Sergeant." I smiled and gave him a generous tip and bade him goodnight.

I never heard my companions come in and I never asked them where they went when we met for breakfast the next morning. Saturday was a fun filled day. We did not arrive at the dining room until ten a.m., having overslept. The Issas had already left and the Huggins had breakfast in their room. The canaries and parakeets were awake and hunting for food. They were quite tame and sat on the sugar bowl waiting for someone to lift the lid. We had a hearty breakfast of juice, melon, eggs, bacon and sausage, toast, marmalade and coffee. My two companions decided to go horseback riding. The horses were trained to climb the mountain and if you were more daring you could ride them down to the beach where they would gallop wildly in the surf. There were bikes available at the hotel, so I took a bike ride along the coast stopping along the way to talk to the natives who had not seen an American soldier in uniform. I stopped at a sugar plantation, made inquiries and was given a tour of the boiler house and the rum-making factory. This gave me a better feel for what Bernadette and her family had to go through toiling in the fields. Coming down from the hill was easy. Going back up was hard labor so I walked most of the way with my bike beside me, arriving just in time to wash up and have a light lunch of a chicken sandwich and iced tea. We then donned our bathing suits and drove to Dunn's River Falls and spent a delightful two hours swimming in the Caribbean and then running over to wash off at the Falls and climb back as far as we dared. It was exhilarating. We had time for afternoon tea served on the veranda outside of our bedrooms. There is nothing as refreshing as High Tea. It was one English tradition that I could easily adapt to. We took a nap and woke up in time for cocktails and then another of Paul's delicious dinners. We were the only ones in the dining room and I wondered how Flora could possibly keep the place going. But she told me that they were pretty solidly booked through the Christmas and January season with families from various parts of the island.

On Sunday morning we went to church at St. Ann's. The priest noticing three American GI's welcomed us during his homily. All heads turned to stare. He invited us in for coffee at the Rectory and we told him how wonderful Father Kiely had been. He knew him well as they had served together before leaving for the Jamaica Mission. We went back to the hotel to say a quick goodbye, to thank Paul, the chef, giving him a generous tip as well as for the waiter and the maid who cleaned our rooms. No wonder they love the Americans. For Flora, I had a surprise, a big bag of delicious MacKintosh apples. She told us that we livened up the place and were well behaved and were welcome at any time. We promised to return. We were refreshed but tired on the ride back to the Fort and made no stops.

Back at the Base the word spread of the delights of Shaw Park Hotel. One of our doctors, Captain Effler, had fallen in love with one of the nurses and they planned to be married in the Base Chapel by Father Kiely. Long courtships during wartime were not practical for the future was so uncertain. They chose Shaw Park for their honeymoon and since McGuire was going to drive them I was invited to go along. I jumped at the chance. The trip was made semi-official in that after we dropped them off at the Shaw Park Hotel, Mac and I would go to Montego and scout out the area for a First-Aid station. The owner of the Montego Bay Hotel was willing to set aside three large rooms on the ground floor for a First-Aid station at a nominal fee. We drove back and had one night at Shaw Park. We picked up the honeymooners and arrived back at the Base. I reported to Colonel Shelley about the Montego Bay site and he said he would have to discuss it with Colonel Ewing. Since regulations did not permit married couples to serve in the same unit, Mrs. Effler was shipped back to the United States. The site of the Montego Beach Hotel for the First-Aid station was approved and plans were drawn to equip one of the rooms with the necessary furniture and utensils and materials for emergencies. The second room with three beds would serve as a hospital ward for those who had to remain overnight or longer, and the other room was for the Corpsmen who would be stationed there. It would be ready by the middle of January, and lucky me I was chosen to be the first to prepare and open the station. An agreement was made with the Jamaican, British, Australian and Canadian forces, that the First-Aid station would be made available to anyone of their men and in particular would be close to any war action on that side of the island.

CHAPTER TWENTY-TWO

BOXING DAY WAS APPROACHING AND all was in readiness for the reunion of Grace and her mother.

Christmas came, my second spent in Jamaica and it is a day even more than Thanksgiving when one wanted to be home. I knew that it was especially difficult for Mom for now my brother Bob was in the Navy serving on the Battleship, *New Jersey*, in the Pacific. My younger brother, Lou, was still in high school and my Gram and Grandfather on my Mother's side were living with us. There would be my Mother's seven brothers and sisters and their wives and their young children all having dinner at our house. So Mom would be kept busy and I knew that would help. I was sure her thoughts were concentrated on Bob and me. After Mass, celebrated by Father Daly, and Christmas dinner, I biked to May Pen to spend the afternoon with Father Kiely and settle the final arrangements. He said that Granny and Grace were at Mass. Granny had not told Grace anything except that they were going for a ride. He wished me luck and said that he would see me at the gate in Spanish Town. I got back to the Base and checked with the chef if all was ready. He and his helpers had packed over two hundred bags with candy, popcorn, nuts, cookies and candy canes. We had taken up a special collection at church for the nuns and our GI's were most generous. One of the nurses had knitted a large colorful decorated Christmas stocking and we stuffed it with pound notes and coins and tied it with a big ribbon. We would give this to Sister Zita to use for goodies for the Sisters for whatever they needed. Before stuffing the stocking I had casually counted the money and it was well over three hundred dollars. This was remarkable considering what little pay the GI's received. Even Colonel Shelley put something in the stocking. I then checked with Lieutenant Weed, who was in charge of the Base orchestra. He was also an accomplished accordion player. We had acceded to Sister Zita's wishes that the band confine themselves to Christmas carols and quiet music. When they last played many of the numbers were pure jazz resulting in the patients leaving the auditorium and dancing themselves to exhaustion outside on the lawn. After we had left that day the poor Sisters had had a difficult time calming them all down. Corporal Wilkes had a beautiful tenor voice and his repertoire ranged from ballads to opera. He along with Weed and his accordion would be the main attractions for the entertainment. Since Pearl Harbor, the whole Fort was on constant alert so that few of the soldiers were allowed to leave the Fort at any one time. There would be only twenty of us this year to make the trip in addition to the band and two of the nurses would join us, Lieutenant Frances Scott and Lieutenant Dorothy Riegle. Anne Hines, director of the Base service club, who worked with the chef in preparing the gift bags and was always willing to help out, and Alice Mulally from the Kingston USO would be among the group.

The next morning, Boxing Day, we left the Base at ten a.m. to allow the Sisters time for the patients to have their medications, treatments and be ready to receive us at noon. Sergeant Mac had arranged for the transportation and we were provided with three Army trucks. One truck was to carry the band instruments, the gifts and the refreshments. Two other trucks were for the men and several jeeps for the others. Mulally was to drive from Kingston and meet us at the Leprosarium. The caravan set off and we drove slowly, for Boxing Day was widely celebrated throughout the island and there were many on the road. Sister Augustine had figured out that it would be best to have Granny and Grace at the gate at two o'clock when everyone would be in the auditorium for the show. The Sisters were waiting for us when we arrived at the Convent and the truck with the supplies and instruments drove into the Compound. The gifts would be given after the entertainment by one of the GI's who would be dressed as Santa Claus. Groups would visit the hospital dormitory to distribute the other gifts to those who were too ill or crippled to attend. The show was to last between thirty and forty-five minutes. Following the show there would be refreshments and a party back at the Convent, given by the nuns. Since Sister Mary Augustine and the other Sisters had spent weeks purchasing over 200 gifts to fit each individual patient and they worked long into the night wrapping each gift, they would be happy to see us arrive and probably happy to see us go as most of the work fell on their shoulders and there were only nine of them.

As we all trooped down to the Compound, Sister Augustine said, "Can I see you a minute, Sergeant? I want to make sure that I have the program in proper order." I knew what she meant and we lagged behind the others.

Sister said, "Everything is planned. After the program in the hall starts, keep your eye on me and wait for a signal. When you see me nod my head, slip out the back. They will think that you are just going to check up on things. Everyone knows that Mary will not attend. It took me a long time to convince her to go along with the plans, but her desire to see her little daughter overcame all of her fears. She will meet us at the back of the Convent and we will go down the road together. I had to bring Cornelius in on this, as he is to relieve the gate man so that he can attend the show. Cornelius is our most trusted friend and will do anything for the Sisters."

"I know, Sister. I don't understand why he does not convert."

She gave me a sharp look. "Cornelius' faith is deep. He believes in God and loves Him and that is all that God asks of any of us." I never brought it up again.

Sister ducked into the Convent and came out with one of the most beautiful dolls that I have ever seen. The face was translucent porcelain in the color of ecru. Long lashes on lids that opened and closed surrounded the brown eyes and the hair, which felt real, was deep brown. The white linen dress was beautifully hand-embroidered with red poinsettias and green ivy.

I gasped and said, "Where did you get this, Sister? You could not have purchased it with what I gave you. It had to cost a lot more."

She smiled slyly and said, "I have my sources."

She reached into her apron pocket and gave me back the five-pound note. She had only been here a few months and already some poor merchant in Kingston had fallen under her spell. Just then Mary came from behind a poinsettia bush and again I was astonished. It was as if the doll had come to life. Mary was dressed exactly like the doll!! There was not one blemish visible on her beautiful face. Sister was delighted with my reaction.

I turned to her and asked, "How?"

She said, "I know how to paint more than furniture."

No wonder she was called Sister Surprise. I found out later that the merchant was Abe Issa. After he returned to Kingston from his visit to Shaw Park where I had told him about my visits to the Leprosarium and the plan for the Christmas party, he contacted the Sisters and asked if he could help.

Sister Zita turned the phone over to Sister Augustine and she told Abe she would be in Kingston within two days on a shopping spree for gifts for the patients and they set up a meeting. She never beat around the bush and told him what she wanted. Sister picked out a doll at one of his emporiums, and then asked if a dress could be made exactly like the doll's dress. She had come prepared with Mary's sizes. When he found out that the dress was for Mary, he was putty in her hands for he knew Mary when she was singing in the Glass Bucket nightclub and was an ardent fan. Abe said that he would have one of his talented women work on it immediately. Abe inquired who the doll was for and Sister said, it was for one of the little girls at the leprosy Compound so Mary's secret was kept intact. When Mary presented the doll to her daughter, Grace, she would be presenting an exact replica of herself. I wondered how she would ever explain the beautiful dress and the makeup to the Sisters and other patients in the Compound, but Sister had that planned out too.

As we approached the gate, Cornelius came out from the little gatehouse and pointed across the road and there stood Granny, dressed in her Sunday finest and holding onto her hand was Grace. When Mary saw them in the distance, she halted and turned as if to flee but Sister grabbed her arm. The iron gate was made of steel bars with openings wide enough to pass through packages brought by those who feared to enter the Compound but not large enough for even the smallest child to slip through. I could not see Father Kiely and looked at Cornelius. He pointed down the road and there parked under a cottonwood tree was Father Kiely's car. When Grace saw Mary and Sister approaching the gate she started to pull away from Granny's grasp. It took all of Granny's strength to keep Grace from fleeing from her.

Sister whispered to Mary, "Remember now. You cannot touch her. If you do I will have to report it."

Grace was crying, "Mommy, Mommy."

Tears were streaming down Mary's face. Sister had done an excellent job for the make-up stayed intact. Granny could no longer hold onto Grace who ran and pressed herself against the iron bars.

Thrusting her hands inside waving frantically she called, "Mommy, Mommy."

Mary thrust the doll through the iron bars into Grace's hands. Holding the doll solved the problem of contact. Mary stood at the gate beyond reach. Granny, too, was crying and was speechless and turned to cross the road. Cornelius moved back into the guardhouse and Sister and I retreated up the road a bit leaving mother and child alone. Mary was kneeling now talking softly to her baby. Soon Grace stopped crying and we could hear the laughter of a child. We could hear the sounds of the orchestra drifting over the Compound, "Joy To The World." After a few moments, Mary stood and beckoned for her Mother to come to the fence and Granny came to Grace's side. Here again mother and child were unable to embrace or to touch one another. Granny started to apologize for not having come sooner but Mary quickly silenced her.

"It is I who must ask for forgiveness. All of the sacrifices you have made, the tears you shed, the worries I gave you and yet you never stopped loving me. It is I who should ask for your forgiveness."

Granny could not speak. Then we heard the sounds of "Silent Night" and Sister knew that the program was coming to an end and that we had to get back. She went ahead of me and whispered in Mary's ear and nodded. Mary kneeled again close to the fence.

I was standing by and I heard her say to Grace, "Mommy has to go now." Grace began to protest. Mary silenced her. "But I will be back soon. When you hold that doll just remember that it is Mommy and we are hugging. The doll's name is Mary."

Mary rose quickly, turned and went back up the path with Sister and me trailing. I could hear the screams of Grace and when I looked back Granny was holding her in her arms. Grace was clutching the doll and kissing it and Father Kiely's car slowly appeared. As Sister hurried on I watched and waved as Father Kiely got out and helped Granny and Grace into the car. I saw Cornelius standing at the guard gate with a large white handkerchief, wiping his eyes.

I slipped back into the auditorium just in time for Wilkes' part in the program. He was singing, "Silent Night." The room was silent. His beautiful clear voice rang out and when he finished, the hall erupted with applause. Then Sister stepped out from behind the curtain. A murmur arose from the audience. What did Sister Surprise have to say?

After they quieted down she said, "I have a surprise for you," and they all laughed. "I have a special guest for you who will sing a song in honor of Sergeant Crouch and all of the wonderful American men and women of Fort Simonds who came here to bring joy into your lives."

The curtain parted and there in front of the orchestra stood Mary. There were gasps from everyone in the audience including the Sisters. She was stunning. She walked over to the piano and the beautiful melody and words from "America The Beautiful" rang throughout the auditorium. As she started the second verse, the orchestra joined in and Wilkes strode over to stand beside Mary and together their voices rang out with the words "Shine thy good with brotherhood from sea to shining sea." At the end pandemonium broke loose. The Sisters were weeping, I was weeping, Augustine was smiling broadly and the orchestra crowded around Mary who looked panic-stricken. Sister went up on the stage and took her arm and led her back to the children's house. Later, when the patients were all enjoying their ice cream, cookies and soda pop, I asked Sister how did she get Mary to consent to perform?

"Simple," she said matter-of-factly. "I told her it was for Sergeant Crouch." She took my hand, "But seriously, Sergeant, she is truly grateful to you and so am I." Then she brightened, "And we pulled it off, didn't we?" I nodded.

Back at the Convent in the midst of the party for the soldiers, Sister Zita asked Sister where she got the gown and the make-up.

Sister calmly explained, "Remember when Mr. Issa called and you gave the phone to me. I had planned a surprise for Mary to sing for the soldiers. I wanted her to be beautifully dressed and Mr. Issa donated the gown."

Sister Zita persisted, "And the make-up?"

Sister Augustine laughed. "Mr. Issa again. I told him that I wanted to put on plays for the patients and a package arrived containing a full make-up kit."

Sister Zita wagged her finger at Sister Augustine and said, "You neither asked my permission nor even told me."

Sister Augustine said, "I did but you probably didn't hear me."

Sister Zita said, "One of these days, child . . ." and then she went and hugged Sister.

We were all exhausted and said our goodbyes.

Sister Zita said, "Sergeant, all of you make us proud to be Americans."

CHAPTER TWENTY-THREE

WE BOARDED OUR TRANSPORT AND HEADED out of the gates. All the way back to the Fort I kept reliving the scene at the gate between mothers and children–Granny and her child Mary, Mary and her child Grace. It reminded me of another Mother standing at the foot of the Cross watching the suffering of her Son. How she longed to hold Him in her arms, wiping away His blood, sweat, and tears, but had to just look and suffer with Him. I could still hear the sweet voice of Mary as she sang those beautiful words "And crown thy good with brotherhood from sea to shining sea." She was a golden canary locked up in a cage.

In the days that followed no one questioned me as to where I had disappeared to during the program nor had anyone any suspicions concerning our little plot. It seemed that all worked well, thanks mainly to Sister Augustine. It was two weeks since our trip to Spanish Town when I heard from Father Kiely. I knew that he was busy with his parish and I did not have an opportunity to bike over to May Pen. He arrived at the Base one day and when we were alone he told me that he had good news. He had been working on this plan several days before we went to Spanish Town. One of his wealthy parishioners, a Chinese merchant and his wife, were seeking someone to care for their two young girls while they went to work. After further inquiry, Father learned that they were not looking for a maid or a cook. They already had them. They wanted someone to whom they could trust their children. The Chinese were very industrious, many were devout Catholics, and their generosity sustained their little church. Father thought immediately of Granny. It would get her and Grace both out of the shantytown and no one loved children more than Granny. The biggest obstacle had been Granny, but on the ride back to Spanish Town he approached her on the subject, impressing on her how wonderful it would be for Grace to be removed from shantytown and live with a normal family. Granny asked if he had told the family about Mary in Spanish Town. Father said that the family had not asked any questions about their background and were pleased that Father Kiely had recommended her and that was good enough for them. They would live in the main house, have their own private quarters and have their meals with the family and Granny would be relieved of any hard work. Granny agreed, realizing that it would be a perfect opportunity for Grace. So Father made arrangements and sent one of his parishioners in a car to pick up Granny and Grace. He did not think it would be wise for him to do so because someone was bound to recognize him and there would be questions. He told me that Granny wanted to see me and to thank me but he assured her that he would make arrangements for that in May Pen. I was overjoyed. Granny and Grace were now safe. I had always worried about them in shantytown where there were many disreputable characters living.

Before he left, he told me that I should stick to my duties and not get involved with schemes or plots any more. I assured him that I had had it but I knew that what he really meant was to keep him out of my schemes. I forgot to ask him if Granny was planning to go to Spanish Town anymore but he had already arranged that. He would take her from time to time without Grace and she could inform Mary of what was happening, no longer involving Sister Augustine nor I.

The days passed by swiftly as other events occurred. An Army bomber had crashed in the swamp. I was part of the rescue team. Then there was the visit of several USO troops, and in particular the visit to the Base by Eleanor Roosevelt, the wife of the President. There was a day when I was aboard a B52 bomber heading for Puerto Rico to take part in a program to develop theatrical programs for the Bases scattered throughout the Caribbean. The plane crashed over the coast of Haiti. (All of these events are described in detail in the book that Sister Augustine and I co-authored, entitled, "Two Hearts, One Fire.")

I visited Granny and Grace several times in the weeks that followed and the transformation in both of them was remarkable. Granny was dressed in a black dress with lace collar and cuffs on her sleeves and wearing black shoes. She no longer wore a bandana and her steel gray hair was held back with a jeweled comb. Grace paid hardly any attention to me as she was busily playing with her new friends. She was finally enjoying her childhood. The two little Chinese girls were six and eight and both they and Grace were dressed alike and except for skin coloring and eyes one would think of them as three sisters. She was now an integral part of their new family and Father told me that the Chinese couple wanted to adopt Grace but Granny resisted. They thought that Grace was an orphan. They did not know that she had a mother locked up in a Leprosarium. They even enrolled Grace with their two daughters in a private Convent School run by two Dominican Nuns. I thought how wonderful Mary would have felt if she could see her daughter. Granny had kept her informed and Mary was now at peace, knowing that her daughter was happy. Granny told me that Grace was so involved with her new playmates and surroundings that she seldom mentioned her mother anymore. At first this hurt Granny but she realized that this is what Mary would have wanted and was content, as she did not believe that Mary would ever leave the Leprosarium.

Mary did not know about the experiments taking place at the United States National Leprosarium in Carville and with leprologists in England. The sulfones came on the scene and a sulfone derivative known, as Promin seemed to show some promise. The new wonder drug of the age, penicillin, had no effect on leprosy. Dr. Muir, the well-known leprologist from England, had visited the Jamaican Leprosarium and had discussed the experiment with Mother and the local physicians. At first the results were not encouraging. The drug had to be given by injection, which was painful and had violent side effects such as nausea, vomiting and high fevers. The harshness of promin was modified by changes in dosage, composition and delivery as experience grew with the medication. Finally, after many years of groping in the dark to find answers to this baffling disease, the door was opening slightly and a ray of light was creeping in.

CHAPTER TWENTY-FOUR

I WAS IN THE STOCK ROOM PUTTING away my freshly arrived supplies when Mac burst into the room carrying a newspaper.

He thrust it at me and said, “Have you seen this?”

I put down the box of bandages and took the paper. “The Daily Gleaner” was the only paper on the island. A two-inch headline ran across the top of the paper MURDER AT SPANISH TOWN LEPER COLONY.

“The nuns?” I almost screamed.

“No, a patient killed another patient,” and he grabbed back the paper. He continued, “I have a car and permission to go to see if we can help out. Do you want to go along? Colonel Shelley said you could if you want to go.”

I quickly took off my green scrub suit and put on my uniform. “Let’s go,” I said. We jumped into his jeep and he tore out of the gate and I held on for dear life and yelled, “Take it easy. That paper is a day old. This thing did not just happen. You will kill us!”

He turned toward me, grinning and said, “It’s an emergency. I have a chance to open up this thing.”

We tore down the highway and turned onto the Spanish Town road. Now he had no alternative, he had to slow down for there were carts and animals and pedestrians. My heart stopped racing.

I asked, “What did the article say? Who was it?” I shouted.

He was gripping the wheel tightly. "I don't know. You know the patients, not me. Some guy by the name of Sylvan chopped up another with a machete."

Sylvan, I thought, big, brutal Sylvan, the kingpin of the Compound. Sister Augustine had once described him to me as a bully. She knew that something like this was bound to happen one day. Everyone in the Compound was fearful of Sylvan and many would not do anything they were asked to do unless they got Sylvan's approval first. One person he was not quite sure of was Sister Mary Augustine. She was careful not to provoke him but she showed no fear when she was around him. He had been a member of a gang on the streets of Kingston and was often in trouble with the law. He had been in prison several times and had escaped. After he contracted leprosy and was confined to the Leprosarium, before the Sisters arrived, he had climbed the walls and escaped into Spanish Town. The police were afraid of him, not because of his brute strength, but because of his disease and he would often go back on his own accord. The Sisters confined him to the Leprosarium jail and he could no longer escape.

We pulled up to the door of the Convent and saw Mother Mark walking in the garden saying her rosary. She looked up surprised when she saw the car stop and hurried over. I thought that she might be annoyed and think that we were interfering but she seemed pleased to see me. We entered the closed patio. As usual, her first thought was whether we were thirsty or not.

I jumped in before Mac had a chance to say anything and said, "No, Mother, we are fine."

Mother looked to Mac, "Are you sure?"

Mac looked at me and then said, "I could use a beer, Mother." She smiled and left the room. I looked over at Mac and glared at him. "I can't lie to a nun," he said mischievously.

Then Mother re-entered the room with a beer and a coke for me. "You have heard the news?" Mother asked.

Mac blurted out, "We read it in the paper, Mother, and the Colonel sent us here to see if we could be of any help."

"How kind of him," Mother said. "Please sit down." After we were seated she turned to me and said, "I'm sure that you want to see Sister Mary Augustine but she is in bed. She is suffering one of her severe migraine headaches and is not well. If she knew you were here I'm sure that she would struggle to join us but I would rather that she rested if you don't mind."

"No, Mother, please don't disturb her. I remember the day that she visited the Base when she had a terrible migraine and was sick to her stomach."

Mother continued, "I am worried about her lately for these headaches are coming on more often. I want her to go to the doctor but she keeps putting me off."

"Did she witness the murder, Mother?" I asked.

"Yes, I am afraid that she was in the midst of it, poor thing. Cornelius' death moved her deeply." She shook her head and tears welled up in her eyes, "We all loved Cornelius. He was such a fine young man and so devoted to the Sisters." She looked at me. "You know that he was a Seventh Day Adventist and was deeply rooted in his beliefs."

I did not want to press on but I was anxious to know and said, "I would like to know what happened, Mother, if it is not too difficult for you."

She took a deep breath and told us what had happened.

"The United Fruit Company had donated to the Leprosarium a plot of land for a farm. They could now grow most of the vegetables needed on the small patches of land on which they had started the farming project. Sister was given charge and mapped out plots on which the many variety of vegetables were grown. Instead of putting one man in charge of the farm she assigned a plot to each man so that they knew the right conditions for each of the different vegetables. This avoided any chance of one patient lording it over the others, which always ended up in an argument. The men had just gone back to the Compound for their lunch and the first contingent of Sisters had also returned to the Convent so there were only two Sisters on duty at the time, leaving only Sister Marina, who was in charge of the kitchens and Sister Mary Augustine.

"Sister Augustine had left the farm and was approaching the Compound when she heard screams. Thinking that the women were at it again, she went there first but they all pointed to the men's side. Sylvan was standing on the walkway, a two-foot long bloody machete in his hands, and lying before him was Cornelius. He had meant to decapitate him but Cornelius had turned to run and the machete caught him in the back and split him almost in half. Sister first rushed directly to Cornelius and knelt down beside him. Cornelius was still breathing and Sister told him, 'Cornelius, you know that God loves you.' He could hardly talk but he whispered, 'S'tah, me knows,' and he took his last breath. Sister was expecting to receive the next blow from Sylvan's machete but he merely stared at her, dropped it on the ground, walked over to the table and began to eat his lunch. Cornelius had often reported him scaling the women's wall at night. The Sisters would punish him by placing him in the cell of the jail on the Compound. The punishment never bothered Sylvan and it never stopped him from his rendevous. After the attack on Cornelius, the men were huddled far away from Sylvan cowering in fear, but one had the presence of mind to run to the office and notify the Sister on duty who immediately rang the emergency bell, which was connected to the Convent. The Sisters knew that something bad had happened and they pushed back from the table and ran to the Compound. In the meantime, the Spanish Town Police were notified. Usually they were slow in coming but when Sister told them that a murder had been committed it was not long before two cars of Constabulary rushed into the Compound, with their sirens piercing the air. Sylvan calmly continued to eat his meal. Sister Augustine stood there and would have tried to tackle him if he had made any attempt to flee. But she heard the sirens and within moments, eight husky Constabularies surrounded Sylvan. He wiped his mouth after taking the last morsel of food and they handcuffed him. He gave no resistance. As they led him away, he spat at Sister. Later they found a list in his bedside table and Sister Augustine's name was second to Cornelius."

When Mother had finished her story we sat there silent for a moment and then I said, "Thank God, Sister used her head and didn't attempt to restrain him."

Mother looked at me and said, "Sister may be impulsive but she is not stupid."

"She is far from that," I said.

Mother smiled, "You know her well." Mother went on, "We have gotten things settled down in the last two days. I can sense the patients are relieved that Sylvan is not with them but they are fearful that he will escape from prison and return."

"Won't the police post someone here to stand guard?" I asked.

Mac piped in, "Our MP's would do it."

Mother said, "We cannot interfere with the Jamaican Government. We can handle it. The police are afraid of the patients. I have just doubled the night watch to two Sisters instead of one. We have been given authority by the police to incarcerate anyone who makes trouble in our jail until they arrive. Most of the time we use it for small infractions and never call the police."

"Are you armed?" I asked.

She did not answer me. She just smiled. "Our guard dogs accompany Sister on her rounds at night and the patients are deathly afraid of them. They are better than any weapon."

However, I found out that the Sister who pulled sentry duty had been taught how to use a gun and there were guns available to them. My image of nuns was far from that of one armed with a gun. I had had little to do with nuns before this since I had not gone to Catholic schools and never knew the swat of the ruler.

Mother seemed restless so I stood up and said, "We have to get back to the Base, Mother, but if there is anything, anything that we can do, please call on us."

She held my hand firmly. "I know, Sergeant, that we can depend on you and our brave soldiers, and I won't hesitate to call if there is anything that I can't do. In the meantime just pray for us and I will tell Sister Augustine that you were here. She will be disappointed that she did not see you but pleased that you came to offer your services."

"Thank God," I said, "that Sylvan did not kill her."

Mother said, "I thank God too, Sergeant. I don't know what we would do without her."

Mac shook Mother's hand and said that he would pray for all of the Sisters and that all she had to do was to lift the phone to the Colonel's office and help would be on its way.

We got back into the car and took off for the Base. On the way home Mac said, "You know, they are braver than we are."

"You can say that again," I said.

"They are braver than you are."

"Don't be so damn smart," I said. "If I told you to jump off a cliff, would you do it?"

He poked me on the shoulder. "You know the answer to that." After a moment, he said, "Do you think any of them will ever get leprosy?"

"Sister Augustine told me about one of their nuns in the Pacific who contracted the disease and lives in a little house outside of the Convent. She is in isolation and does not join in the Community."

"It must be hard for her," he said. Mac's foot pressed harder on the accelerator and the jeep leapt forward. "If I were locked up with no hope of ever getting out I would take a gun and put it in my mouth and pull the trigger," Mac said, as the speedometer climbed.

"Take it easy, take it easy. Take your own life but don't take mine," I yelled. Mac grinned and eased up on the pedal. When I regained my breath, I said, "I remember an experiment that we had in the laboratory once. We were testing behavior and we took some rats and put them in a cage and observed them. At first they fought to get out but then some of the rats just gave up and laid down and made no effort to escape while others kept trying. It is sort of like that there. Some of them just accept the fact that they are locked up from their loved ones while others will do anything to escape."

Mac nodded his head and said, "Yeah, but there is a difference. Where can they go once they escape? They can't hide the fact that they have the disease and many of them are maimed and crippled. They wouldn't get far."

"True," I said. After a few moments I continued, "We just think that the Sisters take care of their sores and their bandages but they do more than that. They are their nurses, their doctors, their teachers, cooks, disciplinarians, judge, jury and police all rolled into one. Some of them may look weak but they have to be strong to put up with all of that."

Mac laughed. "I went to Catholic schools in Boston and I know how tough some of them can be. There was one nun that I would have liked to kick in the shins each time she swatted me on the hand with that damn ruler. But I knew that if I did that, God would have sent a bolt of lightning to strike me dead." The laughter eased our tension.

I thought once that I had a vocation but I now knew that God never called me. I was too filled with vanity, pride and rebellion. In one of our many discussions, Father Kiely once asked me the same question. I told him that I did not think that I was worthy. His reply was, "Who is?" In most of our talks together, despite the bantering, he constantly stressed the power of God's love and forgiveness. I remember in particular one night over snifters of brandy, in his dining room in May Pen, I asked him if he ever was lonely living in this isolated spot, deprived of so many comforts that priests in parishes back home enjoyed. He pointed to the crucifix on the wall.

"No one is ever alone if he believes. I'm sure that there are priests in St. Patrick's Cathedral who have moments of loneliness and doubts whether they have chosen the right path. But if He wants you, you are hooked and you will know if you get His call to follow Him."

It was obvious that I didn't. Father always lifted my spirits by reminding me that no matter what I do, what I become, where I go, God is always with me and that He loves me, despite all of my blemishes and all the times I turned my back on Him. Forgiveness is one of the most difficult things for us to do, but not for God. It rids us of hate and revenge.

Then my thoughts turned to Sylvan. Could God forgive him for what he did? Two days before he was hung, he wrote a letter to the Sisters asking for their forgiveness. He thanked them for all that they had done for him and the sacrifices they made to help him in his disease. He was now aware of the harm that he had done during his life and he deserved the punishment that awaited him and only hoped that God would forgive him. I realized that in the end the only one who can really judge us is God Himself.

As we turned in through the gates of the Base, Mac said, "Where were you?"

I looked at him and said, "What do you mean?"

"For the last ten minutes I felt like I was driving alone."

"Oh, I was just thinking," I said as the car came to a stop.

"Well, if you are planning something, keep me out of it."

I watched as the car sped off. If I had never been sent to Jamaica, I thought I would never have met so many wonderful people like Mac nor would I have known about those suffering from leprosy, or the wonderful Angels of Mercy who cared for them and especially my newfound cohort, Sister Mary Augustine. I turned and went back to the hospital.

CHAPTER TWENTY-FIVE

I WONDERED WHAT GOD HAD IN store for me. Had all of this been planned, or was it just a series of coincidences? Only time would tell. Battles were intensifying on both the European and the Pacific fronts. Every man, woman and child in the United States was engaged in the war effort. Thousands of young men and women were entering the Services as volunteers or draftees and had to be trained before they were sent into the war zones. There were continuing changes at the Leprosarium. Every time I visited they showed me a new building and the dilapidated and decrepit ones that I saw when I first arrived were disappearing. With each sign of progress, the Legislature was more forthcoming with funds.

News of all of this progress reached the authorities in the National Leprosarium, Carville, Lousiana, and the British Leprosy Association and its medical staff and leprologist were visiting on a more frequent basis. This pleased the Governor and the Health Department. They were now proud of the progress at Spanish Town where once before they neglected the problems. Sister Augustine's school was progressing nicely and had moved from pews in the church to the old recreational hall. The enrollment jumped, as more and more of the older patients wanted to learn how to read and to write, especially when they saw the youngsters making such progress. Alice Mulally took an interest in the library and her volunteers at the USO were donating more and more books.

The Franciscan Nuns, who operated one of the finest private schools for girls in Kingston, also helped out with supplies.

The school was not the only project that Sister Augustine was engaged in. It seemed that she had her fingers in every pie. The new farm took a great deal of her time, as did all of the new construction. She was an expert in drawing up plans for the new building. Every piece of the new building was drawn to scale to the amazement of the builders, who had been sent in by the government. Able-bodied men patients were also utilized as their carpentry skills improved. They were busy building desks and furniture. Mother Mark wanted to build a new auditorium. She felt that many of the leprologists who were coming to visit the Compound wanted to hold Seminars explaining the new drug therapy to members of the Health Department. In addition, the auditorium would serve as a new stage and theatre for the patients to put on their own productions which Mother Mark was very interested in. All was planned to lift the patients' morale. Now that Sylvan was gone and executed and no longer a threat, a calm descended over the Compound. The patients were more willing to participate in the Sisters' activities.

There were still many squabbles but none serious enough to call in the Constabulary. I was present one day when an argument broke out between two women. I thought that they were going to come to blows but Sister just smiled. This was routine for her. One woman was blocking the way into the recreation hall.

Finally, one of them had enough, drew herself up haughtily, and said to the woman blocking her way, "Sew up your lip, m'dear, and let me pawse."

I almost doubled up in laughter and the blocker moved out of the way. What a wonderful way to say shut up, I thought. I would have to use that expression when next I got into an argument.

The new kitchen was a marvel with a new stove, utensils, pots and pans, and tin plates, all under the supervision of Sister Marina. Once we found that she carried a gun under her habit we nicknamed her pistol packing Momma (but not to her face). With the new farm there were plenty of vegetables for the table. One of the Sisters, having been brought up on a farm in Nebraska, had great success in raising chickens, goats and even rabbits. The chicken coop and rabbit pens were well insulated from the crafty mongoose. The goats were a little too big for them. Rarely did they serve beef which the patients would not have liked since they had grown so used to goat meat. On special occasions they served 'Am and Haigs.

The new sulfone, Promin, was still causing problems as some of the patients refused it because of the painful injections, but there was a modicum of hope, which raised the spirits of many of the patients. A Dr. Faget in Carville who developed a new sulfone that could be taken in capsule form was conducting experiments and he was eventually successful, creating the drug Dapsone, which revolutionized the treatment of leprosy. Those patients who were responding to the new sulfones would be discharged after three negative smears from tissue fluid taken from the earlobes where the bacilli could be found in the millions. The problem was where did they go when they were discharged? Many of their families would not take them back and they would be ostracized in their communities. It was not unusual for a patient to beg the Sisters not to discharge them. They were living better under the loving care of the Sisters then they would back at home.

Mary was responding to treatment since they had caught her leprosy in its early stages. Granny had visited her several times and Mary told her that soon she would be discharged and would be reunited with Grace. While Granny was overjoyed, when I next met her in May Pen, she took me aside and expressed her fears. The family, to which Grace had now become an integral part, would never accept Mary since they were fearful for their own children, and it would mean that Granny and Grace would have to leave. Where would they go? Would Mary ever be able to work and support them? I told Granny to put everything in God's hands and not to worry and He would take care of it. I think she doubted me but she said that she would try.

CHAPTER TWENTY-SIX

IT WOULD BE MY THIRD Christmas in Jamaica, the second for Sister Augustine. We reverted to the original plan to have my Mother and her group purchase the Christmas gifts. Last year it was too much for the Sisters who had so many other things to do and they were happy with the new arrangements. But, instead of purchasing clothing and the like, my Mother's group would confine the gifts to practical items, such as toiletries and embroidery material. The Sisters would continue to buy the toys for the children since so many were damaged in shipment and it was difficult for my Mother's group to wrap them.

Changes were constant at the Base. A new Commanding Officer and staff, several new doctors and nurses, replaced the more seasoned and experienced ones, who were sent to where there was more action. Fortunately for me, Mac was still at the headquarters. We continued to hold our daily drills and every other month held mock war exercises, involving landing on the beach in full battle gear and there still were fifteen-mile hikes to keep us in shape. Most of the surgery was routine except for one soldier who during a war exercise was shot. Another, while on leave one night, was attacked and suffered a fractured skull, which required delicate brain surgery.

Then came a blow, with the announcement that Father Kiely was being transferred to the Cathedral in Kingston. What would happen to Granny and Grace? Will we have to tell the new priest about Grace's mommy in Spanish Town? After a short consultation with Father, we decided to let things lie and not inform the new priest. Granny and Grace were well established with the family now and unless Mary was discharged, there would be no need to inform Father Eberle, the replacement, of the circumstances. But I would miss Father Kiely, as I did not get into Kingston as often as I had in the past but it was a big promotion for him. He would be living with a fine group of Jesuit priests and brothers. He would have less financial worries and would also teach at the college.

On one of my visits to the Leprosarium in October, they were making good progress on the new auditorium. Sister showed me the plan she had mapped out. The main auditorium would seat 150 patients. The stage would be raised 4½ feet from the floor, affording a good view. It was 30 feet long, 15 feet in height and 10 feet in depth with two dressing rooms off one wing and two storage rooms for equipment leading from the other. To the rear of the auditorium was a raised platform one foot from the floor, surrounded by a balustrade, with seating for 40 people. This was for visitors who would not need to sit with the patients. That's all the details that Sister would give me. She had other surprises up her sleeve and once the auditorium was completed it was sealed from view from all but Mother Mark, Sister Zita, and a handful of workmen. It was then that I was given the sad news that Mary had failed all three of her tests. The leprosy still showed positive. Sister told me that at first she was depressed but when she was informed that they were making good progress in Carville, her hopes were raised again.

Boxing Day arrived, and we came to the Leprosy Compound with the gifts, the band, refreshments, and Santa Claus. This time the program had been changed. The patients, with the Band and Soloist to follow, would present the first portion of the program. When we came to the auditorium the patients were already seated. Some visitors from Kingston were in the visitor section. I was ushered to a front row seat in the patients' section and was seated next to Vitel Bennett who always served as Master of Ceremonies. He was in his 60's. His disease was arrested but he could not take the harsh treatment of Promin. Like most Jamaicans, he loved to give speeches. On the other side sat Mother Mary Mark. The first surprise was the beautiful red curtain that draped across the front of the stage, hanging from a gilded proscenium. I looked at Mother and she just nodded knowingly. Where did Sister get all of that material and how did she possibly hang it, for I knew that it must have weighed several hundred pounds. In front of the curtain was a series of footlights.

I turned to Mother and was about to ask her, when she said, "In time, Sergeant. In time."

She was enjoying the mystery. Soon the soldiers joined the visitors. The shutters covering the windows on both sides of the auditorium were closed but they were slanted, leaving room for the breeze to blow through the auditorium. The ceiling lights dimmed, a hush fell over the audience and through loud speakers attached to a record player came the sounds of the theme from "Gone With The Wind." Mother was beaming. I was flabbergasted. Then the curtain rose to form a beautiful drape like effect. How did she ever do that? I wondered. Then came gasps, cries, "Oh Laudy, Laudy, Oh, Oh's" and applause. The stage was bare but across the back wall on a canvas that stretched 30 feet in length and 10 feet high was a magnificent scene of a walled garden. The wall was topped by potted ferns at strategic points with a bright blue sky beyond and silhouetted against the sky were the tops of palm trees. I immediately recognized the wall. It was a duplicate of the wall that surrounded the Compound. In front of the wall were shrubs, trees, and beds of all of the flowers that grow in

Jamaica, hibiscus, poinsettias, hollyhocks, roses of every variety and color, forsythia, and ferns of every size and description. In the center, a stone path led to a tall fountain spouting streams of water. Everything was scaled to the proper dimension, giving a three-dimensional effect so that one thought that they were actually walking through the garden. Then to the sounds of "The Nutcracker Suite" three girls entered from the wings of each side of the stage. They were dressed in dresses of a silky material with many different colors and attached to their backs, a multi-colored butterfly wing. They danced gracefully as if they were flitting from flower to flower. Could Radio City do better than this? I thought. The rest of the patients' program was composed of Jamaican songs, dances and skits. The skits brought howls of laughter from the patients. They knew what was going on but the GI's were confused with the dialect. The final scene was that of the Nativity. Kneeling around the Crib, containing a doll resembling the Infant, was Joseph in full robes and beard and Mary in beautiful blue and white. I immediately recognized her as Grace's mommy, Mary. There were shepherds and angels and even a live donkey. I noticed that Mother left just before the last scene and I imagined that there was some emergency, but when the lights came up on the Nativity there were seven nuns dressed in white gathered around the piano. Their beautiful voices lifted in harmony singing, "Joy To The World." As the curtain dropped, some of the patients were startled to hear loud whistles coming from the GI's in the visitor's section. Then came the applause and the stomping of feet. Their hands were almost blistered as everyone stood in a standing ovation. I thought of Lieutenant Weed. How could we top this? We might as well pack up the instruments and head back to the Base. There was a twenty-minute intermission as several GI's lifted the piano up onto the stage and the band prepared for their part of the program. They remembered that at a previous Boxing Day Concert they played a great deal of Jazz and once the patients took up the beat the auditorium was emptied. The GI's all thought that they were dissatisfied with the music. But no, they were all out on the lawn, sashaying to the music, twisting and twirling and some even dropped to the ground in exhaustion. After we left, the poor nuns had had a difficult time restoring normality. So this time they had prepared winter music, both religious and secular, and Wilkes sang "White Christmas." This time the swaying took place in the auditorium and shouts of "Hear! Hear!" came from the patients. After the performance, there was much milling around Sister Mary Augustine.

I heard Vitel Bennett, the self-appointed spokesman for the patients, say to her, "S'tah, you are an artist fer sure. It all look so real dem bees keep coming to de flowers."

No one could have said it better. Sister kept pointing to Mother, telling them all that it was her idea. She was but the instrument. After Santa Claus passed out the presents and the GI's distributed the ice cream, cookies and other goodies, there was a complete air of festivities. After the reception back at the Convent, we wended our way back to the Base, happy again that we had brought a little sunshine into the lives of those who live so much in darkness. I did not know it then but it was to be my last Christmas in Jamaica.

CHAPTER TWENTY-SEVEN

THE WEEKS AND MONTHS PASSED by uneventfully. I no longer biked to May Pen since Father Kiely had been moved to Kingston and for the first time I was beginning to feel homesick. It had been more than two years since I had seen my family. Mom wrote faithfully, always enclosing $2.00 from her cookie jar. She told me about the rationing and the difficulty of obtaining butter and other foods. Fortunately, my Father had a steady position as an engineer on the Pennsylvania Railroad and even during the darkest days of the Depression, he still had work. While she worried about me, it was my brother Bob who was in the most danger as he was serving on the Battleship *New Jersey.* More and more battles were fought as we tried to re-take the islands that had been lost to the Japanese. Each battle was bloodier than the last, including Iwo Jima, Bougainville, and Guadalcanal. While I was in Jamaica, the only real danger I faced was a bite from a scorpion.

One day Colonel Shelley called me into his office. He said nothing. After I saluted, he pointed to the chair in front of his desk and I sat down. He then handed me the paper, which contained my orders to return to the United States for a 30–day leave and a reassignment. It did not state where I was to be reassigned.

Colonel Shelley said, "I am sorry to lose you, Crouch. But I know you are itching for a change."

"How long do I have, Sir, before I will be leaving?" I asked, feeling exhilarated, depressed and afraid.

"You have ten days. Time enough for you to visit your friends in Spanish Town. They will miss you too." He looked up at me. "I will see you in 30 minutes in the O.R., we have a hot appendix to take out."

That is how he dismissed me, a man of few words. I stood, saluted, turned and left his office. I was tempted to go to May Pen to see Granny and Grace for the last time, but goodbyes were not my strong point. So I thought that I would just let it lie. I did what I could and it would be bad enough to say goodbye to Grace's mommy when I saw her at the Leprosarium.

I telephoned Mother Mary Mark and she was deeply sorry to see me go and asked when it would be convenient for me to come and say a last goodbye. I told her that I could get away on Saturday, two days before I was to leave.

She said, "Oh my, that doesn't give us much time."

Knowing Mother, I knew that it would not be a simple goodbye so I said, "Mother, please do not go to any trouble. I just want to say goodbye to the Sisters and the patients and assure them that they will not be forgotten. I have already spoken to Mac, who is still here and he promises that as long as he is here, there will be a Boxing Day Party."

She said, "That's good news. I will tell everyone. I am sure that they will be pleased." Then she hesitated, "I may not be able to tell you this in person so I want to let you know that Sister Augustine has not been feeling well."

"Oh," I said. "Is it serious?"

"When you see her, please don't mention that I said anything to you or even make a comment about the way she looks. She is very sensitive about this and she is ignoring the doctor's advice. I could force her to be obedient but I think in time she will realize that she will need more sophisticated treatment than we can give her here."

"Is it the migraines, Mother?" I asked.

"The doctor thinks that she might have a brain tumor," Mother said and I could feel the tension in her voice.

"I hope that she doesn't wait too long for if it is a tumor it can grow and spread, you know," I said.

"She hasn't lost any of her functions, no paralysis, no tremors and her vision doesn't seem to be affected. Her ears bother her. She insists that it is just headaches and she continues to push herself. I know what is going on inside," Mother said.

"She doesn't want to go back to the States."

Mother said, "Right. You have hit it on the head, Sergeant. I know if she leaves here she will not return to the Missions, which is the main reason she joined our Order. I know I can count on you not to bring it up. It will all work out in the end. I am confident of that." Her voice sounded brusque as if she was giving me an order. "Until Saturday, then. When I tell everyone the news of your leaving, they will be sad. God keep you in His care," and she hung up.

CHAPTER TWENTY-EIGHT

MAC SAID THAT HE WOULD DRIVE me on Saturday. When we arrived at the Leprosarium, Mother and Sister Zita were waiting outside of the Convent and took us directly to the Compound. This was strange, I thought. Usually we went to the Convent first. When we arrived at the Compound everyone was in the new auditorium. Mother told me that they had had little time to prepare any formal celebration. I was grateful for that, I told her, as I hated goodbyes. As we entered the auditorium everyone shouted, "Hear! Hear!" a typical British acclamation and I was led up onto the stage where several chairs had been arranged. It was a simple ceremony with the long speech by Vitel, expressing the gratitude of all of the patients. The highlight of the short musical interlude was little Corny. He had been left at the gates of the Leprosarium when he was but five, abandoned by his family. He was an imp in every way and was the darling of the Compound and of the Sisters as well. Always up to some mischief. He was now seven and was dressed as Uncle Sam, minus the beard, and to the recording of George M. Cohan's "Yankee Doodle" he tried to tap, gave it up, and ended with a Jamaican version to the squeals and applause of everyone. The song ended and Corny kept dancing until one of the Sisters came and led him offstage. Shades of Shirley Temple, I thought. He would have been a Hollywood star. I shook as many hands as I could and hugged others and went from ward to ward to say goodbye to those who were too ill to come to the auditorium. Fortunately, Mac, ever thoughtful, ever faithful, had brought several large tins of cellophane wrapped cookies, which I distributed.

As I said my last goodbyes and we headed back to the Convent, I noticed that all of the other Sisters had disappeared and Sister Augustine and I were alone. I had been wondering how I could get to talk to her privately.

I said, "Sister, where is Mary? I did not see her anywhere."

Sister Augustine stopped and looked at me. "She is too upset, Sergeant. She is wondering who will watch over her child now that you are gone, even though she is aware that Granny and Grace are now in good hands with the newly adopted family. She depended on you to be there if any emergency would arise."

"She is typical of many people in the theatre that I have met," I said. "In the spotlight they are full of confidence and eat up the attention they get, but basically many are shy."

"Like you," she said, not sarcastically.

"Thanks a lot," I said.

"Well," she said, "you know that this is like a little village. There is no privacy here. Everyone knows everyone else's business and Mary felt that she would break down saying goodbye to you and it would send tongues wagging."

"I would have liked to have had a few words with her."

There was a strong breeze blowing that ruffled her veil. She said, "I will take care of that."

I looked at her, "How do you know what I want to say?"

She looked at me. "I know you better than you think," and she hesitated, "Brudder."

I stopped. "Brudder? What do you mean by that?"

She flushed. "I think of you as a brother and that is what I call my brother. I hope you don't mind?"

Now I felt myself redden. "I'm honored, Sister." We walked a little further on. "You know, I only have two brothers.

I never had a sister. I don't mean to be disrespectful but would you mind if I called you Sis?"

"Brudder and Sis, it is." We shook hands and she laughingly said, "Only in private." I knew what she meant.

We were nearing the Convent when I took a breath and said, "How are you feeling?"

She looked at me sharply. "I'm fine, just fine," she said emphatically and I knew that was the end of the conversation.

The sound of a piano and much chattering came from the enclosed patio of the Convent. The puzzle as to where all of the Sisters had gone was answered. We entered through the screen door to much applause. I was surprised! The patio was gaily decorated with red, white and blue streamers. There were tables of food and refreshments and I gasped as I saw Father Kiely, Alice Mulally, Cissy Rowe and her daughters, Punky and Betty, Colonel Shelley and several of the nurses.

When I approached Colonel Shelley, I saluted and he said gruffly, "None of that."

He put out his hand and I took it. He said in a low voice, "Don't worry about me. I will watch my language in front of the Sisters." I laughed.

The Sisters had gone to great lengths and must have dipped deeply into the budget for there was sliced turkey, sliced chicken, ham and even roast beef, potato salad, coleslaw, Boston baked beans, which I saw Father Kiely take several helpings of, pickles, potato chips, beer, punch, lemonade, rolls and butter, all served on red, white and blue paper plates and napkins. On one small table was a large square cake covered with white frosting. In the center in red, white and blue icing was an American flag and across the top was written, "Thank You, Sergeant Crouch." How could the Sisters have done that? I thought. Oh well, I stopped being surprised. One of the Sisters was playing the piano as everyone sang familiar tunes and gorged themselves with the delicious buffet.

Then came time to cut the cake and Mother turned to Colonel Shelley and said, "We are grateful to the Colonel and the chefs at the Army Base for this beautiful cake. When they called me to offer it in the spirit of a Missionary, I quickly accepted the gift."

Everyone laughed and I cut the first slice. For all of his gruffness and swearing, I thought underneath he was a softy. Finally, Mother rapped for silence and introduced shy Sister Zita. I knew that this was hard for her.

"You know how words are difficult for me," she said. "We are all happy for Sergeant Crouch to return to his home, but we are sad at this parting. We have all become friends, Sergeant, the patients, the Sisters, the Jamaicans you have come to know, and your Army buddies. So now, I am exercising my authority," and everyone clapped. "I have asked someone special to sing my favorite song, which tells like no other what friends mean to one another."

Sister Micheline picked up her violin and when the door to the Convent chapel opened, Mary entered the room. She was dressed in Irish kilts and walked to the piano. A hush fell over the room, and tears sprang from my eyes and then came the haunting sounds and words, "Oh Danny Boy, the pipes are calling." The words poured forth slightly tinged with an Irish brogue from Mary's throat. There was not a dry eye in the place as the last words were spoken almost in a whisper. There was a long moment of silence and then the applause came in wave after wave. Mary came over to me, kissed me and walked back into the chapel and closed the door.

To break the somber mood, Mother Mark said, "Let us all join hands and sing not just to the Sergeant but to one another," and the pianist struck up the strains of "Auld Lang Syne."

As we all departed there were more goodbyes.

Father Kiely blessed me and said, "You are like a bad penny. I'm not going to say goodbye. You will show up again."

They all lined up outside of our car and before I entered it, I turned to Mother Mark. I hugged her and gave her a loud kiss on the cheek. All of the nuns clapped and my face was as red as the hibiscus that lined the driveway. As we drove off, I turned to look back and kept waving until we had passed through the walled gates and down the dusty road to Spanish Town.

CHAPTER TWENTY-NINE

AFTER A FEW MOMENTS, MAC turned to me and said, "Open the window and stick your head out."

I looked at him and said, "Why? You want my head to be cut off by a passing cart?"

"No," he said mischievously, "It's swelling and it will break through the roof."

Nothing like your own kind, I thought, to bring you down to earth.

We were fairly silent for a long way before he spoke again. "Those nuns, they really surprise me. I have the whole station at my disposal and I have a hard time getting supplies. Where did they get the lights, the Uncle Sam costume and the kilts?"

I turned and looked at him and said, "You are used to nuns. You ought to know by now that anything they want, they get. They have a way about them. Sister Augustine told me that she got all of the stage lights and footlights from a friend in Boston and the Sisters celebrate all of the American holidays. The Hibernians in Boston sent the kilts for St. Patrick's Day, and the Uncle Sam outfit for the Fourth of July. They came in handy when they were preparing the farewell for me in such a hurry."

Mac was silent for a while. "I'm going to miss you, Crouch," he said. "We have shared good times together."

"No, we will not say goodbye because I know we will meet again in Scollay Square." We both laughed.

My thoughts quickly turned to Mary, Granny and Grace. I probably would never see them again. I prayed that Mary's leprosy would be arrested and she would be able to leave the Leprosarium to renew her life with her mother and her daughter. There was nothing more that I could do. It was all in God's and Our Lady's Hands but I knew I would never forget them. Mac, like the good friend that he was, sensed my silence as I gazed out at the passing countryside. As we passed the sugarcane fields, the trees, the huts, the goats and the mountains in the distance, flashes of pictures as if taken by a CAT Scan, passed through my mind.

My first day when I arrived in Jamaica, my arrival at the Army Base, my first glimpse of Grace sitting by the roadside, the days of packing and organizing the hospital, the sick calls, the dispensary, the operations that clicked by one by one. Then came the images, the wonderful Jamaican friends that I had made. Kathleen and Leonard Swaby, the Rowes, the men, women and children at the Leprosarium, the wonderful nuns in white from Massachusetts, and the many Jesuits who had taken me under their wing. I had spent three years on this magical island and it was now a special part of my life. I would carry these images until the day the last picture would pass from my brain. I was more convinced than ever that God had put all of this in His plans for me. I did not know the future. I was returning to a country still at war, neither Germany nor Japan had surrendered as yet. I would be going home, seeing my family for the first time in three years. Would I be able to adapt? And after my leave where would I be sent? What would happen to me? I was prepared for whatever was to come. I was not aware that tears were trickling down my cheeks.

Mac spoke up. “What was the name of that little girl that you took such an interest in?”

I did not hear him. The CAT Scan was just beginning to wear down.

He poked me in the shoulders, “Hey, Hey,” he shouted. “Come on back.”

Startled, I turned to him. “Oh,” I said. “Sorry, what did you say?”

“I said,” and his voice was sharp, “what was the name of that little girl that you took such interest in? Where were you for the last few minutes?”

I laughed. “A private place,” I said. “I go there once in awhile.”

“OK,” he said. “Then don’t answer my question. You know that I outrank you and I could order you to answer, but with your connections it would all probably boomerang on me.”

I settled back in my seat, put my head against the headrest and closed my eyes and I said softly,

“Her name is GRACE.”

EPILOGUE

AFTER SEVERAL DAYS, I BOARDED an empty oil tanker headed for New Orleans. The Army used any method of transportation available to them. I spent two days in the fun loving city and then boarded a troop train and headed for Fort Dix. Soon after my arrival, I was given a 30–day leave of absence and left for my home in New Brunswick, New Jersey, which was 30 miles from the Fort. The leave of absence passed too quickly as I had not seen my family and friends for three years. Mom cooked all my favorite meals and my waist expanded. I luxuriated in the freedom to do what I pleased, and when I pleased.

I received orders to report to Camp Barkley, Texas and was assigned to teach Medical Corpsmen the basic elements of First Aid. I hated it and was relieved when I was assigned to the hospital ship, *Larkspur*, based in Charleston, South Carolina. After a brief course in physical rehabilitation at Washington and Lee University in Lexington, we set sail empty to cross the Atlantic at a slow pace. The ship was white with a huge Red Cross painted on either side and we were lit up at night so that U-Boats could identify us and hopefully obey the Geneva Convention. At first, our destination was Southampton, England, but after D-Day we were routed to Cherbourg, France to pick up the wounded. During the trip home we would replace the bandages of the wounded soldiers and change their casts. Over the ship's loudspeaker I would give lectures on what would happen to them once they returned to the States. They would be dispersed to various rehabilitation hospitals and if possible, would be made ready to return to their units. I was at sea on both V-E and V-J day and after the Japanese surrendered I was discharged from the Army.

I took advantage of the GI Bill and entered Columbia University where within the next four years I was granted a B.S., M.A., and M.S. degree in Hospital and Administrative Medicine.

I was anxious to make a return trip to Jamaica and in 1948, I sailed aboard a freighter from New York to Havana and after two days in Cuba I took a plane to Jamaica. I spent most of my time with Father Kiely and revisiting old friends, Kathleen and Leonard Swaby, Cissy Rowe and her daughters Punky and Betty, and many others. The USO was closed and Alice Mulally had returned to her home in Chicago, but we kept in touch by mail. I was anxious to visit Spanish Town to see if I could find out what happened to Grace, Granny and Mary. Father Kiely said that he had lost track of them since he had moved from May Pen to the Cathedral in Kingston.

The Marist Sisters sent a car for me in Kingston to bring me to the Leprosarium for a full day of activity. They had not forgotten me. Sister Mary James was now the Superior. Shortly after I had left Jamaica Sister Augustine returned to the States, convinced that she needed specialized treatment. After many tests they discovered that she did not have a brain tumor but the root cause of her headaches was infected mastoids. She underwent several radical operations, resulting in a great loss of hearing. After being greeted by the Sisters, I asked Sister Mary James if Mary was still a patient. She told me that Mary had responded very favorably to the sulfones and had been discharged. She had gone to May Pen to claim her daughter and then left for England but no one knew her whereabouts. Granny had remained with the family in May Pen. Not long after Mary left for England, Granny passed away.

Later on in Kingston, at dinner with Leonard and Kathleen Swaby, Leonard told me that he had been able to obtain papers for Mary and Grace to travel to England. Granny's two brothers, who had left the plantation when they were young to return to England, had both established successful businesses and Mary was to join them. Leonard did not have Mary's current address. I was content to know that mother and daughter had been reunited and were living, what I hoped, was a happy life.

I made many other trips back to Jamaica but by then one by one death had claimed my friends beginning with Father Kiely who died suddenly with a massive cerebral hemorrhage. On another trip, Leonard Swaby was gone. Followed by Cissy Rowe, Kathleen Swaby and Cissy's daughter, Punky. Betty had moved to Texas and I still correspond with her. On each return trip I found profound change in Jamaica. Hotels crowded every inch of the shore surrounding the entire island. Jamaica had gained its independence. I had experienced the pristine beauty of this jewel of the Caribbean, which was now losing much of its natural attraction. The Leprosarium was finally closed and the Marist Sisters had returned to the States. The remaining patients were cared for in the local clinics and hospitals. The Army Base was abandoned and given to the government of Jamaica. Much of the beautiful city of Kingston had turned into slums. Gangs roamed the streets making it unsafe to wander. Finally, it had lost its lure for me and I have not been back in more than 25 years.

The saga of Grace, Mary and Granny is still fresh in my mind. When we last met, Grace was but a little girl, full of charm, capturing much of the beauty of her mother. Mary's voice still rings in my ears. Then there was Granny, tall, erect and dignified with her clay pipe between her lips. Granny, I knew, was gone. Mary must be in her eighties, Grace in her sixties, yet in my mind I see them as a little girl, a beautiful young woman and a dignified elderly lady. On Halloween, when the ragamuffins ring my doorbell, seeking treats, I scan them to see if Grace is there. In church I will listen, as hoping to hear the sweet notes of Mary's beautiful voice. Time has erased much of that, but in the writing of this book all of the images were sharp and clear as if it all happened just yesterday. I hope one day we will all meet again, little Grace in a patched dress, a bright red bandana on her head, hunched over a bowl of mangoes. Granny will be along the riverbank, scrubbing my uniforms and beating them against the rocks, Mary no longer caged within the walls of a Leprosarium, and Father Kiely, whose friendship and sharp Irish wit, helped to make lonely nights more bearable. Leading them all will be Sister Mary Augustine, my collaborator for more than fifty years. Now in Paradise she will welcome me with her infectious smile, greeting me with the words,

"Hi! Brudder."

LEPROSY PERSPECTIVES PAST, PRESENT AND FUTURE

by
Wayne M. Meyers, M.D., Ph.D.
Registrar for Leprosy and Chief, Mycobacteriology
Armed Forces Institute of Pathology
Washington, District of Columbia
and
Research Affiliate
Tulane Regional Primate Research Center
Tulane University, Covington, Louisiana
Member, Board of Directors
Damien-Dutton Society

LEPROSY: PATIENT CARE AND RESEARCH

INTRODUCTION AND BACKGROUND

From time immemorial there have been numerous efforts to manage and control leprosy. While these efforts were usually well intentioned, they often went awry. Such were the attempts to halt the leprosy epidemic that began in Hawaii in the early 19th century and rapidly swept through the islands. King Kamehameha V on January 3, 1865 approved an act to prevent the spread of leprosy, to "secure the isolation and seclusion of such leprous persons as . . . may by being at large, cause the spread of leprosy." The place chosen to secure the seclusion was on a peninsula of the Island of Molokai surrounded on three sides by rough seas and on the fourth by a high pali (cliff). This peninsula was made up of three sections: Kalaupapa, Kalawao and Makanalua. The first patients landed on January 6, 1866. Arthur Mouritz, in his book, *The Path of the Destroyer*, published in 1916, recounts one consequence of this act in what he called "The Leper War on Kauai." This one-time physician to the "Leper Settlement" on Molokai states that Sheriff Hitchcock of Kauai (known by the sobriquet "The Holy Terror") told him: "If leprosy can be stopped by getting all the lepers to Molokai, I propose to keep going after them until I get them all."

Life as a patient on Molokai in nearly every respect was deplorable, but far from unique. Robert Louis Stevenson, the Scottish novelist, poet and essayist in the latter 19th century, from his own observations wrote, "There are Molokais all over the world."

In 1886, Father Damien, undoubtedly the best-known figure in the annals of the history of leprosy, sent a poignant report about the leprosy patients on Molokai to Walter Gibson, President of the Board of Health in Honolulu. This document occupies 18 pages of Mouritz' book and is entitled, "A Personal Experience: Thirteen Years' Residence and Labor among the Lepers at Kalawao." The social and moral degradation that Damien found in the community of patients and their helpers on his arrival May 10, 1873 is best summarized, as he stated, in Hawaiian, "Aloe kanawai ma keia waki" ("in this place there is no law"). Thirteen years later in his 1886 report, Damien was able to write, "I am happy to say that . . . my labors here, which seemed to be almost in vain at the beginning, have, thanks to a kind Providence, been greatly crowned with success, as at present, there is very little, if any at all, of the . . . evils committed."

Those who have had the privilege of visiting Kalaupapa and Kalawao will remember vividly the collection of patent medicine bottles retrieved largely from the lava tube caves by Richard Marks, recipient of the Damien-Dutton Award for 1996 and a long-time resident of Kalaupapa. These bottles originally contained the vain hopes of scores upon scores of patients for a cure. After all, the only treatment they had available were a "few physics and their own native medicines." Damien, however, was a man of vision, and stated, "Perchance, in the near future, through the increasing interest and untiring perseverance in the study of the disease by the most intelligent physicians and scientists, a proper specific for the cure of leprosy may be discovered, which to my knowledge has not yet been found." Damien did not live to see the day he envisaged; however, his life—so deeply devoted to compassionate care, punctuated by acts of political activism—raised the social conscience of the world toward the stigma of leprosy and pleaded for the mitigation of this stigma. Damien's death from complications of leprosy on April 15, 1889 secured his name forever in the chronicles of the struggle against leprosy.

EARLY RESEARCH

Just before Damien's arrival on Molokai, G. Armauer Hansen in Bergen, Norway, began to pave the way for the modern understanding of leprosy. Hansen was convinced that leprosy was an infectious disease and not, as many of the scientists of the day believed, either hereditary or simply an adverse response to environmental factors. To prove his postulation, Hansen examined numerous specimens of tissue fluid from the skin of leprosy patients, and on February 28, 1873 recorded his belief that the microscopic brownish "sticks" or rods he saw were the cause of leprosy. This landmark in the history of microbiology launched the quest for the scientific understanding of the disease that many years later would lead to the realization of some of Damien's hopes for leprosy sufferers. Hansen's discovery took place nine years before Robert Koch cultivated the tubercule bacillus in Berlin, Germany. The leprosy bacillus (*Mycobacterium leprae*), thus, was the first germ known to cause chronic disease in humans, and was the first of many findings in leprosy to contribute to biomedical research on other afflictions (e.g. complications of diabetes).

Even though Hansen was unable to grow the leprosy bacillus in test tubes and was not successful in infecting animals experimentally, the scientific community accepted his concepts on leprosy as a contagious disease. The Proceedings of the First International Leprosy Congress held in 1897 in Berlin contains reports on the status of leprosy in many endemic countries. By then the widely accepted infectious nature of leprosy reinforced measures for isolation of leprosy patients—"preferably on an island"—to control the disease, and it was further recommended that "healthy children should be separated from their leprous parents as soon as possible." Lacking effective chemotherapy, these measures may have reduced the prevalence of leprosy in the more affluent countries but had very little, if any, influence on numerous socio-economically deprived countries where leprosy was more highly prevalent.

MODERN ERA OF LEPROSY CONTROL AND RESEARCH

During 1900–1940, commensurate with the modest technological developments in biomedical research in this period, the control and understanding of leprosy progressed little. The 1940's brought a new and exciting era in patient care, ushered in by the bold efforts of Guy Faget at Carville, Louisiana, who after careful long-term observations established the efficacy of intravenous sulfone in treating leprosy. By 1947, Cochrane had shown that a more convenient oral form of sulfone, called dapsone or DDS, was highly effective. This drug was inexpensive, it withstood harsh tropical climates and was relatively nontoxic. More than a decade would pass before this "miracle drug" was employed widely. Gradually, however, DDS brought revolutionary changes, liberating many patients from both the physical damage and the stigmatizing sequelae of leprosy. Ambulatory treatment programs gradually replaced domiciliary care, markedly diminishing the stigma and the social disruption of the lives of patients and their families. Patients could now live at home and visit the treatment center periodically, or mobile units could go to satellite clinics along roads or paths. One by one leprosaria began to close, but more frequently, the leprosaria became reference centers and provided care for the severely disabled. During this same era, pioneering surgical rehabilitation, coupled with injury-preventive measures for insensitive hands and feet, permitted patients to lead happier, more productive lives. The renowned orthopedic surgeon Paul Brand spearheaded this remarkable effort.

Many proactive groups over the years had called for abolition of the term "leper" to help minimize the stigma of leprosy. Improvements in treatment and management of patients helped their cause. One important outcome in this movement was the following resolution approved by the International Leprosy Association in 1948 in Havana:

"That the term 'leper' in designation of the patient with leprosy be abandoned, and the person suffering from the disease be designated 'leprosy patient.'"

Others, notably Stanley Stein, Founding Editor of *The Star*, the patients' publication at Carville, preferred the designation "Hansen's disease" or HD for leprosy. Successive staff members of *The Star* have remained faithful to Stein's policy. Many authorities, however, retain the word "leprosy" for the disease, and "patient with leprosy" for those who have the disease.

Beginning with Hansen in 1873, numerous investigators attempted to grow the leprosy bacillus in the laboratory, without success. John Hanks, for example, spent his long professional career in pursuit of this elusive goal of leprosy research, in laboratories from Culion in the Philippines (1941–1945) to Harvard University and finally Johns Hopkins University.

Failure to achieve cultivation of the bacillus obstructed studies aimed at understanding the organism, and made it all the more important to develop models of the disease in animals. Based on observations by Chapman Binford at the Armed Forces Institute of Pathology, Washington DC, in the late 1950's, leprosy infections were established in experimental animals during the next two decades. Infections in mice became the standard for testing chemotherapeutic agents and revealed the important discovery that leprosy bacilli were becoming resistant to DDS. In the early 1970's, Storrs, Walsh and others at Gulf South Research Institute in Louisiana, found the armadillo to be highly susceptible to leprosy. This salient discovery opened new avenues of leprosy research by providing large numbers of leprosy bacilli for an amazing array of leprosy-related scientific studies in, for example, diagnostic reagents, pathogenesis, epidemiology, chemotherapy, immunology, vaccines, and molecular biology.

For what many view as unfortunate missed opportunities, research on the pathogenesis and treatment of experimental leprosy in the armadillo was never sufficiently funded to reach its enormous research potential. Nevertheless, as a spin-off, the armadillo opened new vistas in the epidemiology of leprosy: newly captured animals often already had leprosy, indicating that there were nonhuman sources from which humans could contract the disease, discussed more fully later in this chapter.

PRESENT STATUS OF LEPROSY, AND PROSPECTS FOR THE FUTURE

With the above background we will proceed to several topics of current interest in the battle to control leprosy. Some of these subjects are controversial. While others often share the views expressed here, unless otherwise indicated any opinion that appears polemic is the author's responsibility.

Chemotherapy with multidrug regimens

The report of sulfone-resistant leprosy in 1964, and the subsequent discovery that such resistance was virtually universal, made therapeutic alternatives imperative and urgent. While several other antileprosy drugs were already in use, combined regimens were not employed. The pioneer multidrug therapeutic trial was undertaken in 1973, by Depasquale and Freerksen in Malta. Their regimen contained dapsone, prothionamide, isoniazid and rifampin, and proved to be effective.

In 1982, the World Health Organization (WHO) issued their recommendations for Multidrug Therapy (MDT). These recommendations were based on carefully considered but empirical judgments of efficacy, applicability in field programs, and cost. Goals were to, 1) treat patients, 2) prevent bacterial resistance and 3) interrupt transmission. The primary drugs employed were dapsone, clofazimine and rifampin, administered for fixed periods of six or 24 months depending on the form of leprosy. Treatment would then be stopped and the patient removed from official registries as a leprosy patient, whether or not there were sequelae such as deformity and/or disability.

Cooperation between WHO, voluntary agencies, and the governments of endemic countries was excellent. Based on the above criteria, in 1991 WHO reported that the number of leprosy patients worldwide had dropped from a previously estimated 10–20 million to 5.5 million, a remarkable achievement in any light. These statistics prompted WHO to approve a resolution in May 1991 to " . . . attain the global elimination of leprosy as a public health problem by the year 2000." Elimination as a public health problem was arbitrarily set at one patient or less per 10,000 population, by country. WHO data in 2002 indicated that, compared to 1981, the prevalence of leprosy was reduced by more than 90%. Currently the global prevalence of leprosy is slightly less than 1 per 10,000 population and 83% of the patients live in 6 major endemic countries—India, Brazil, Myanmar (Burma), Indonesia, Madagascar and Nepal. WHO sets the total global number of leprosy patients today at approximately 800,000. Many authorities, however, estimate that the total number is 2–3 times higher.

WHO's goal of the elimination of leprosy as a public health problem by the year 2000 was not achieved. However, special strategies were established to aim to achieve this goal by the year 2005: 1) elimination campaigns to reach hidden cases, 2) action programs to reach patients in all readily accessible areas, and 3) provision of MDT to every general health facility. At the same time there are attempts to reduce the maximum duration of treatment to 1 year, and even to 1 month or less. If such reduced duration treatment programs become acceptable and present WHO guidelines for patients with active leprosy are maintained, prevalence rates will approach the number of new patients "successfully" treated per year. Potentially, this could lead to the somewhat absurd interpretation that leprosy had been conquered.

The stated accomplishments to date of the WHO's program of the "elimination of leprosy as a public health problem," unfortunately, has had certain results that have negatively impacted leprosy programs: for example, leprosy research today is meagerly funded, if at all, in most research institutes; treatment programs are now being increasingly integrated into general health services that do not possess the special expertise in diagnosis and treatment required for leprosy, and both the public and the medical community are beginning to view leprosy as a solved problem.

One little known risk of a summary approach to the management of leprosy is the potential for misdiagnosis. To economize resources and personnel, clinicians are not being encouraged to take skin smears or biopsy specimens to help establish diagnoses or to guide clinical treatment. Our files in the Leprosy Registry of the Armed Forces Institute of Pathology contain many specimens that represent recent misdiagnoses by clinicians. A cavalier approach to the diagnosis of leprosy is never good medical practice. There is little question that there are fewer leprosy patients now than several decades ago, and that for most patients the quality of life is significantly improved. Much of this can be attributed to concerted efforts to reach more patients with effective drugs. This is most laudable. In view of our present knowledge, however, are we yet in possession of sufficient accurate data to suppose that by 2005 A.D. the goal set by WHO can be reached? Many individuals and some agencies deeply involved in the care of people affected by leprosy believe this possibility is remote. For example, do the reported national prevalences of leprosy represent the real prevalences? Valid data on this question are difficult for many endemic countries to generate. The number of new patients each year (incidence) has declined very little, even in regions where MDT has been rigidly applied for many years, and remains at about 600,000–800,000 new cases each year worldwide. Thus, the goal of the interruption of transmission of leprosy is not being realized. Also, there is insufficient data to assume that there will not be a significant number of relapses following MDT treatment, especially if the period of therapy is reduced to 1 year or less.

Given the relative vacuum of hard data that would withstand rigorous critical analysis, those who proclaim the "elimination of leprosy as a public health problem" must consider their decision very carefully. When "success" is finally announced, will support for leprosy related programs then be withdrawn by WHO? Will national programs be diminished? Will voluntary agencies experience still further reductions in resources to support care of leprosy patients—both active patients and the millions of individuals who remain disabled by the disease? Are those in authority to do so willing to take this step as soon as the year 2005? I hope not, or only if they possess compelling hard data to answer the questions that more and more critics are raising on this issue. Premature reductions in the struggle against leprosy for the sake of a calendar deadline may well spell disaster, and leave our posterity with an enormous health problem, as similar concepts did for tuberculosis.

Eradication of Leprosy

The motto of the XV International Leprosy Congress in Beijing in 1998 was wisely phrased, "Toward the Eradication of Leprosy." This wording was chosen with the belief that eradication is probably a long way off. There are many unknowns. For example, are there significant nonhuman sources of leprosy? What are the most important modes of transmission? Is a vaccine feasible? Can the presumed current trend of reduction of patients be sustained with diminishing resources? Are there modes of control of leprosy other than chemotherapy?

In consideration of this latter question there are two significant historic correlatives: 1) endemic leprosy disappeared from northern Europe long before specific chemotherapeutic agents became available, and 2) no infectious disease so far has been eradicated by chemotherapy. The beginning of the disappearance of leprosy in northern Europe coincided with quantum improvements in housing and other socioeconomic factors in the Renaissance period. Today, socioeconomic status and prevalence of leprosy in most regions are inversely proportional, suggesting that improved housing and other living conditions will reduce or even eradicate leprosy. Further, if the most important route of transmission is the nasorespiratory passages, as most authorities believe, then more spacious dwellings would reduce contagion.

We now know that there are nonhuman sources of leprosy bacilli. A high percentage of armadillos in the southern United States are naturally infected with leprosy bacilli.

Some wild nonhuman primates (monkeys, chimpanzees and possibly baboons) in West Africa and the Philippines have naturally-acquired leprosy. These animals may serve as reservoirs that could perpetuate endemic leprosy in spite of all efforts to eradicate the disease in humans. Some investigators believe that the leprosy bacillus may survive in soil, although this is not widely accepted. At any rate, the role that nonhuman sources of leprosy may play in efforts to eradicate leprosy in humans has been investigated only superficially.

Candidate vaccines for leprosy have long been tested in large field trials, and found wanting. Nevertheless, there is currently a renewed interest in vaccines for leprosy, stimulated by recent developments in the immunology and molecular biology of leprosy and the bacillus that causes the disease. Repeated BCG vaccination confers significant protection against leprosy and may have use in high-risk individuals. The effect, however, seems insufficient to consider BCG as part of a leprosy eradication program.

In conclusion, the struggle against leprosy must go on until all people affected by the disease can live happy and productive lives. Currently there are approximately 3 million people with leprosy-related disabilities, in addition to those with active disease. Today specific national programs for leprosy control and management have been largely dismantled. Many believe that this step is premature, but this is the "real world" of leprosy care. Measures must be undertaken to train all relevant medical and paramedical personnel in the diagnosis and management of leprosy. I do not believe that this is being achieved at an acceptable level, and may be the greatest need in leprosy related activities today. There is still much to do.